"Watch out, half-wit!" she said, glaring at a 'copter that was passing too close. Sylvie touched the controls lightly, and the 'copter faded beneath them, close enough to make Zeke's eyes bulge. "Get a groundcar, dummy!" she yelled.

Bones cleared his throat. "It's so soothing."

"What is?"

"Flying with you, Sylvie. I mean, gosh, you're so calm, so relaxed, so—"

"Holy crow!"

She jerked the control stick and the hoverjet ducked out of the way as a fat green flitter zoomed right at them out of the mist. "What, is there a bull's-eye painted on this thing?"

Bones was twisted around in his seat, looking up and back at the flitter. "There's nobody piloting that thing, Sylvie. It's a robot...and here it comes again!"

DR. BONES ™

BOOK 3:

Garukan Blood

by Thomas Wylde

A Byron Preiss Visual Publications, Inc. Book

ACE BOOKS, NEW YORK

For Quohog

Special thanks to David M. Harris,
Mary Higgins,
Susan Allison,
and Beth Fleisher.

This book is an Ace original edition, and has never been
previously published.

DR. BONES
BOOK 3: GARUKAN BLOOD

An Ace Book/published by arrangement with
Byron Preiss Visual Publications, Inc.

PRINTING HISTORY
Ace edition/April 1989

ISBN: 0-441-15674-6

10 9 8 7 6 5 4 3 2 1

The future is air,
    the House of the Unborn.
The present is water,
    the House of the Living.
The past is earth,
    the House of the Dead.
    —*Garukan proverb*

Sundown on Garu'ka, as the orange star Epsilon Eridani dropped behind the dark-green forest horizon. Keelor Ru shuffled from the site of the dig, coughing in the cloud of fine white dust that the workers kicked up. Ru was designated the junior scientist that day so he was last in line, moving slowly, still half hungover from the night before. He was thinking about that bottle he had hidden in his tent back in camp.

"Hurry up, Ru," yelled one of the guards. He waved his shotgun, and the gaping muzzle hesitated just a fraction of a second too long, pointing at Ru's wide barrel chest.

Keelor Ru frowned. Even the guards were getting nervous. "Hey, I'm on your side."

"Just clear the site, pal," said the guard. "Suppressor fields are coming on early tonight. You wanna fry?"

"Is something up?"

"Just rumors."

Keelor Ru nodded. Rumors. Every dig site had rumors, but usually they concerned what fossils were showing up in the sifting screens—not who was going to attack the workers.

The last of Epsilon Eridani dropped from sight, and the shadows of tall trees covered the ground. Brilliant floodlights snapped on, washing the site in a white glare.

Keelor Ru turned to look back, startled by the way the landscape jumped into focus under the scrutiny of the powerful lamps. Fold after fold of strata lay exposed across the plain, the book of time spread out horizontally, dragged from the depths by the building of volcanic mountains. Keelor Ru smiled, filled with a profound sense of awe at the scientific process—and promptly tripped face first into the powdery dust.

"Hurry up!" said the guard.

Ru swore, snorting dust from his nostrils. When he looked up the guard was standing over him, his wide Garukan chest reflect-

1

ing the light. A trickle of sweat crawled out from beneath his body armor. "You wanna get us killed?"

Another guard sauntered up, squawking into a radio mike. Keelor Ru just wanted to lie there in the soft dust until his head stopped pounding.

"What's the hold up?" asked the supervising guard. "You hit him? What'd he do?"

"I didn't hit him. He fell down."

"I tripped," said Ru, climbing to his knees.

"Clumsy," said the guard.

"They're holding the suppressor field," said the supervisor. "But they don't like it."

"Get up!" said the guard.

Keelor Ru was crawling around on the ground. "Wait a minute."

"Archeologists," said the supervisor. "Every time they fall down they look to see what tripped them. Always hoping to find—"

"What's this?" said Ru, flicking at something hard embedded in the dirt. He grabbed a brush out of his pocket and began to sweep the dust away, very slowly.

"Look at him now," said the supervisor. His radio began to snore, and he spoke into it. "I *hear* you. Hang on, we're coming right now."

"No, we're not," said Keelor Ru. "Call Dr. Darma. Tell him we got a skull here."

The guards bent close.

Beneath the moving brush, the bony brow was emerging, millimeter by millimeter.

"Oh, hell," said the guard. "Dinner's gonna be late tonight."

CHAPTER 1

"I don't care *what* you heard," said Keelor Ru. He waved his glass, spilling a kind of green whiskey. "No matter what, these bones are gonna change the world."

The bar was crowded with noisy folk, and he had to shout to make himself heard. It occurred to him, rather vaguely, that he ought to be a little quieter. Dr. Darma had said something about keeping the bones a secret. But hell, how could you keep something like this quiet?

"Nobody knows exactly what they mean yet," he said, leaning toward the woman with the crooked smile. "Hell, most of 'em are still a part of the ground."

"How old?" asked the woman. A red-faced man beside her seemed not to be paying any attention. Humans, they were . . . tourists, probably.

Ru said, "More than two million years—that's about a million, Earth standard. At least."

"Imagine that," she said. Her companion yawned into his drink.

"Least a million!" said Ru, glancing around. He wanted to talk about the strata, how they had the fossils bracketed by known, dated strata . . . but now he wasn't so sure. He noticed, again rather vaguely, several hard looking gentlemen sitting at a small table against the wall. More humans. They held full drinks and seemed to be watching him out of the edges of their eyes. *They* weren't tourists.

What if Dr. Darma had sent out guys to make sure nobody talked about the bones? Keelor Ru frowned, said, "Uh-oh."

The woman beside him smiled. Now her companion seemed to be watching him out of the corner of his eye. Ru frowned some more. Something was wrong. He slid off his bar stool, and the booze in his glass sloshed onto his shoes. Damn, everybody in

3

the joint seemed to be watching him now. I'm going crazy, he thought.

"Be right back," he said, moving off toward the can.

"Hurry up," said the woman. "I want to hear more about the bones."

"You bet."

Down the dimly lit hall he stumbled, sobering fast, through the kitchen and out the back. The last thing he remembered seeing in the crowded bar was the small table against the wall, and the two full glasses that had been abandoned there.

About this time, fifteen hundred kilometers west, Bartholomew Charles sat in the back of a limo with local industrialist Warren Kingsmill, watching a middle-aged Garukan female limp toward the entrance to an unlit alley. Charles said, "Is that her?"

Kingsmill grunted. "Dr. Darma went through the medical files himself. Sheila R'meel, age forty-six standard, one hundred forty-two centimeters, thirty-seven point four kilos, unmarried, works as a packer in one of my assembly plants."

"She's the one with the roommate, right?" said Charles. "A human female of similar age?"

"Uh . . ."

Bart Charles frowned. Kingsmill was the only member of the Consortium to break away with him, the only one not afraid to act to save his investment in this planet. Charles needed his contacts. "Don't fold on me, Kingsmill. There's a lot of money involved."

"I know that. I've been here twenty-five years. Not like you—"

"I may be new here," said Charles, "but my money's just as good, and my risk is just as great." What he did not say, and what Kingsmill had no way of knowing, was that Charles had already protected his investments. Seeing a full-scale rebellion as an almost certain occurrence, whether his current, desperate plan worked or not, he had been secretly arming both the planetary government and the rebels. Small arms at first, with the promise of more lethal weapons if the fighting escalated. So Charles would make a dandy profit if war broke out. If, by some remote chance, peace broke out instead, he would use his and Kingsmill's contacts to take over the Consortium. Bart Charles liked to play high-stakes games, but only if he held all the cards.

Charles pointed to a figure crossing the street a half a block away. "There, Kingsmill. Tell your . . . man."

Kingsmill got on the radio to the car in front. "The one with the limp," he said. "See her, Manel?"

The radio hissed, then Manel Baviera climbed out of the front car, looked up and down the deserted street, and loped after the female.

Charles raised his nightscope and leaned forward to watch the kill.

Ten minutes later they took the roommate, too. It was a nice match.

Dr. Darma gagged when he saw the two females lying face up on the autopsy tables. Bart Charles stepped into the light, pushing the x-ray machine aside. "What's the matter, Darma? I thought you knew what we had in mind?"

Darma stared at the naked bodies, and all the blood seemed to drain from his face. "Oh, no . . ."

"We need bones, right?" said Charles. He grinned and handed Darma a power scalpel. "Well, they're in there someplace. Get busy!"

Kingsmill laughed from the shadows, a high-pitched, almost hysterical sound. His eyes were shiny, reflecting the light on the autopsy tables. Drunk, probably. Darma envied the man. He took the buzzing scalpel and moved toward the first table.

Don't think about it.

Last stop.

While the hoverjet sat in the clearing, engines smoking, Oakley Clark dragged the box into the tall grass. There were two shovels in the box, but fat chance any of those guys in the 'jet would get out and help.

Oakley grabbed a shovel and stomped the blade into the grass. Not happening. It was like trying to shove your fingers through concrete.

"It's too hard here!" he yelled at the 'jet.

There was a silence, then someone yelled, "Just get it done, Oakley."

"Yeah, thanks," he muttered.

He tried again to force the blade of the shovel past the grass and into the volcanic ash, but it was impossible. "Damn it!"

Oakley dragged the box across the field, pushing down the sharp-bladed grass. As soon as the edge of the box cleared the tips, the grass sprang up, tough as ever. Back on the mainland, the natives built houses out of this stuff.

He tossed the shovel back in the box and walked away, looking for another place to dig. It was dark, and there were things moving in the grass, making slithering, stealthy noises. "Oh, man . . ." He wanted this over with. In a few seconds, with great relief, he broke out into the clear again. It was a dirt road, rutted, half overgrown, but there were twin strips of bare dirt—treated, like the landing circle, to keep the grass down.

Well, hell, dirt was dirt, and nobody ever came out this way anymore—not since Mount Falluu had gone active again. Oakley looked behind him, where the dark bulk of the volcano rose up, covering the stars. He grabbed the box and dragged it through the grass to the road. Here the digging was easy, and he had the box filled to the top in no time. He thumbed the starter, got the box up in the air a few centimeters, and angled the thrust until it floated back toward the 'jet in the clearing.

This was the last, the fresh volcanic ash. The river silt, the sand, the limestone powder, all were aboard, boxed up and ready to go. Not such a bad night after all.

And the money was great.

They made the rendezvous in plenty of time, and Dr. Darma seemed to like the dirt a whole lot. Weird guy, but then, not much of this made sense to Oakley Clark.

Some weeks later, after considerable trouble—and quite a bit of good luck—Bart Charles leaned back in his temporary office in the capital, getting comfortable. On the screen Dr. Darma paced endlessly, waiting to show the fakes to Professor Elliot. Charles leaned forward and keyed the mike. "Will you stop that?"

"I'm nervous," said Darma, glancing in the direction of the hidden camera. "What if he doesn't believe—"

"Shut up!" said Charles.

The fossils were *perfect*. Anybody would be fooled. Even the famous Dr. Ezekiel Bones. Hell, these fossils were going to drive Bones crazy.

He smiled.

The door to Darma's lab swung open and Professor Elliot

limped inside, wiping his glasses on his shirt. It had been a lot of trouble keeping him away from the dig site, but they needed somebody who thought the bones were real. Elliot was perfect. He hardly noticed Darma on his way to the table and the precious bones. The professor's smile was beatific. It was love at first sight.

Carlos Janova sat blindfolded in the wobbly chair and patiently tried to explain. "I don't know if the bones are real or not. All I know is Professor Elliot is satisfied with them."

"They cannot be real," said the rebel leader, the one Janova knew only by his raspy voice. "If they're real . . . it's hopeless. The fossils will be seen as proof of our descendence from hominids and we'll never get the humans off our backs."

"I know that," said Janova, "but I can't change the facts. If the bones are real, you'll have to get by the best you can."

"No one will get by."

"They'll kill you," said Janova. "If you try it, they'll squash you flat."

"So what?"

"How can you say that?" Janova squirmed in the wobbly chair, utterly frustrated. It was so pointless, fighting now. No way could the humans keep up the pretense. The government had to fall soon, taking with it that pack of well-paid politicians whose signatures had made life so pleasant for the Consortium the last fifty years. "They know it can't last," said Janova. "The government, the Consortium, everybody knows it can't last. Garukans are no more descended from humans than maggots from garbage."

"So now we are maggots? You've been working for the humans too long."

"Listen to me," said Janova. "I can bring my friend to Garu'ka. He's a scientist, an archeologist. If the bones are faked, he'll know it. If the proof you need is still in the ground, he'll find it. You can trust him."

"Who is he?"

Janova told him.

The rebel leader laughed. "You're crazy. He's human . . . and he's rich. How could I ever trust him?"

"You trust me?"

"So far."

"I don't have to be here, telling you this. I could be killed."

"By us!"

"Yes. And by them, too."

"That's true."

"So: you trust me . . . and I trust Dr. Bones."

Janova heard no answer, just incomprehensible whispers, and the sound of footsteps on the gritty wooden floor. It was the first time he realized they were not alone in the forest cabin. "Look," he said, "all I'm asking is that you postpone your attack. Wait until you see what Dr. Bones can do."

"I don't know," said the man with the raspy voice. "The longer I wait, the stronger the government will become."

"Bullshit, they will always be more powerful than you. If you fight, they'll destroy you. And worse, our cause will be damaged. If the bones are faked, this will come out eventually. If our ancestry is real, it will be proved eventually. But if you fight now—even if you later prove your case—the Council will take forever to make the transition. The humans will say we are violent and irresponsible—and they will be right."

"This is our planet! They can't take it from us!"

"Face it, they already have. And if you want it back, you're going to have to be patient."

The rebel leader was silent a long time, and Janova wished he could pull his blindfold off. How can you convince someone if you can't see his eyes?

"All right," said the voice. "Go fetch your Dr. Bones. We'll see what he has to say."

"If it doesn't work," said Janova, as a joke, "you can always kill me."

The Garukan laughed, but it was no joke.

"Carlos Janova," said Bart Charles. "I just got word he's left for Earth. He's gone to get Dr. Bones. You understand what this means?"

The white-haired man nodded. He looked a lot like Bart Charles, but it was no coincidence. Charles liked the idea of having surrogates run errands for him.

Charles said, "Take my ship. I don't care how you do it, but get there in time to catch Janova at the spaceport. Kill him. Kill him before he can talk to Bones. And if you can't be sure, kill Bones. I can't have him coming here, not now."

Again the man nodded.

Charles looked away. "Be subtle, if you can. Keep me out of

it. A long time ago Bones got my son killed. People remember that. If anything were to happen to him, folks might suspect me. Try to be discreet, but get it done."

Keelor Ru was lying drunk in a sleazy room in Squall City, on the outskirts of the Great Wilderness. His bottle was empty, the bar was closed, and it was too late to go back out on the street tonight. It was too late to do anything.

He closed his eyes and thought about the bones. Screw Dr. Darma, with his secrets and his dirty money. The bones were safe. All he had to do now was figure out who to give them to.

If the corrupt occupational government got hold of them, that would be the last anyone would ever see of them.

As for the rebels, who knew what they'd do with them? They were all crazy, stoned on political desire and self-righteousness.

This was science, damn it. You couldn't let the politicians get involved. They all had their plans, their agendas, their vital programs. To them, the truth was just something you worked with, like wet clay.

Those bones belonged to the people of Garu'ka—the same people he had almost betrayed. He'd taken money to keep quiet, and there was supposed to be even more money later. Well, he wouldn't see any of that, not after stealing the bones from Darma. He wondered if they knew yet. Probably.

Things were heating up. There was a rumor someone had left Garu'ka to bring back Dr. Ezekiel Bones, said to be a man you could trust. Maybe. If he came at all.

In a room down the hall it sounded like someone was trying to flush a holovision cube down the toilet. Just another happy customer in the bitter night. "What's your *problem*?" Ru yelled. The noises stopped, but the silence was worse and the bottle was still empty. The fear was back, sitting on his wide Garukan chest. They were out there somewhere, the men he'd double-crossed, waiting for him to show his face.

Keelor Ru was on the run. He just hadn't got very far yet.

CHAPTER 2

Carlos Janova was already dead as he stumbled off the helipad's safety zone. He just didn't know it yet.

Outside in New Haven Core City II a chill rain was falling from a spring afternoon sky thick with darting hoverjets and slower moving cargo 'copters. Under the campus domes of New Yale it was warm; students and visitors hustled to and fro, under the bright artificial sunlight.

It was all lost on Janova as he struggled toward a downlevel ramp. His world had withered and turned gray, the voices of the class-bound students sounding distant and blurred. He didn't notice the way they looked at him, pointing at his bloodied face and torn clothes.

He stumbled down the endless ramps, moving blindly, hoping for help but unable to ask for it. When at last he focused his eyes, he saw he was on Level Six. It meant nothing to him. Where the hell was Bones?

Janova blundered into the wall and slid to the concrete. His legs quivered, going numb, but he forced himself back up. His mind kept replaying the same images: the men who grabbed him outside the spaceport, the car screeching to a stop at his feet, its doors already open, more men reaching for him . . . all those hands in his face, punching and tearing at him . . .

"Watch it, buddy," said a student, as he dodged around the stalled Garukan.

"Wait," Janova whispered. "I need to find . . ."

The student didn't hear. Dozens more passed by, intent on making it to their next class on time. They looked at him, smiling strangely, and moved on.

Janova leaned his cheek against the cool metal wall. His body jerked with physical memories: thrashing arms, straining legs. He could see the curb where he lay—just for a moment, staring at a shiny red candy wrapper—before the rough hands pulled him up. He broke free and ran, hard as he could . . .

When he opened his eyes, the hallway blurred and swayed. His leg refused to move. Janova closed his eyes again and waited. I'll start again in a minute . . . in just a minute. . . .

A mechanical voice began to call, polite but insistent. "Sir? Sir? Sir?"

Janova opened his eyes. A corridor monitor stood before him, its amber plastic eyes scanning him. Janova tried to smile. "I seem to be stuck."

The robot quivered on its wheels, appearing impatient. "You must not loiter in the thoroughfare, sir. There is a public lounge on Level Seven."

Janova shook his head. It hurt. "No," he whispered. "I have to . . . find . . . Dr. Bones . . ."

"I presume you mean Dr. Ezekiel Bones," said the robot. "At this moment he's lecturing in . . . Lecture Hall Six-E. Down this hall, turn right, third door on the left."

"Wait . . ."

"Excuse me?"

"I'm going to need some help . . . getting there . . ."

"Of course, sir." The robot sprouted arms and grabbed Janova as he slid down the wall. "Is Dr. Bones expecting you?"

Janova lied. "Yes, yes . . . of course . . ."

"Very well, sir," said the robot, as it hustled the drooping body down the hall. "But you realize I cannot allow you to interrupt Dr. Bones until his lecture ends."

Janova almost laughed, but he hadn't the strength. To have come this far . . .

Lecturing in person, as usual, Dr. Ezekiel Bones roamed the aisles of the amphitheater, finishing his thoughts on the ethics of archeology. "So there were the British, just bursting with pride. What a marvelous business it was! Let other men grub about in Africa and Asia, pawing the earth for man's fossil remains. Let them have their Java man, their Peking man, their African bones of nameless troglodytes. Mother England had her own to champion—Piltdown man."

He paused and looked about. Most of his hundred or so students were awake today. It was the next-to-last lecture of the term, a time when the attendance swelled with the deadheads who'd signed up months before and decided, rather late in the game, it was time to make a good impression.

Ezekiel Bones smiled, thinking of the surprises some of those students would find in their computer records.

"Piltdown man," he repeated. "Discovered by solicitor Charles Dawson in a gravel pit in Sussex, not so very far from London. And, for a while, it looked pretty good: well-aged brown bones, parts of a skull and a nice jawbone. And the skull was huge—of modern size, though the jawbone looked as primitive as an ape's. Oh sure, there was some controversy. All the other fossils—Java man, Peking man, Heidelberg man—all had smaller skulls and more modern jawbones. But what the heck, this was Britain's own: *Eoanthropus dawsoni*. It was unfortunate that—"

Zeke frowned at the perplexed faces he was seeing and stopped to spell out the name. "*Eo, anthropus*: dawn man. Dawson's Dawn Man." Some of the students made written notes, others just tapped on their computers. When the activity had died down, he went on.

"Unfortunately, the bones were too precious to be tested much. It took years for scientists to discover the file marks on the teeth, where the orangutan's jaw had been worked on. Dawson had painted the surface of all the bones with potassium dichromate, giving them a fine brown patina. The only genuine bones found scattered about the pit—some ancient animal bones— were hopelessly out of date compared to the gravel where they were found. An examination of fluorine in the teeth—well, you get the idea. Read the text."

Zeke started back down the steps of the amphitheater, his long legs taking them two at a time. "Piltdown man was a hoax that lasted forty years because folks found it pleasant to believe what they wanted to believe instead of digging in there and finding out what the hell was actually going on."

Zeke stepped behind his lectern and glanced at his notes on the inset screen. A Q-light flickered on the seating chart. "Question, Mr. Bata-bukini?"

A young black man rose in the third row. "Sir, this incident occurred more than five centuries ago. Certainly you don't mean to suggest it could happen again."

Zeke smiled. "Granted it would be more difficult—but while the science of fossil dating has advanced, there has been little corresponding progress in correcting man's ability to fool himself and his fellows."

"That's a rather gloomy assessment," said Mr. Bata-bukini.

"Nevertheless."

Another seat light was glowing.

"Miss Grdinich?"

A plump young woman, her skin tinted a fashionable green, sat up straight. "Dr. Bones, there have been rumors of something found on Epsilon Eridani Two . . ."

Zeke grinned. "A controversial site. The inhabitants call it Garu'ka. Yes, I've heard the rumors."

Miss Grdinich nodded vigorously. "So is it just a coincidence you're lecturing on ethics—and the Piltdown affair in particular —just as news arrives that—"

Zeke's eyebrows went up. "Don't you believe in coincidences, Miss Grdinich?"

"Not around you."

With that the chimes sounded, and Zeke said, "Okay, that's it for today. Try to make it next time. Friday will be, as you well know, the final lecture of the term."

Someone yelled, "Are you gonna have our papers graded by then?"

Zeke smiled. "Come Friday and find out. I may surprise myself."

Students were climbing down the aisles and filing out, cassette screens flickering with final notes and reminders. The green-skinned woman stopped in front of Bones as he was packing his briefcase.

"Are there any openings on this summer's expedition, Doctor?"

"No students this time," he said. "Sorry."

"Too hot, isn't it?"

"Pardon me?"

"Garu'ka. The whole thing's about to blow, isn't it?"

"Blow up, politically—I guess you mean."

"At least. Physically, too—if all those weapons go off at once."

Zeke nodded. "The place is a mess. But what makes you think I'm going to Garu'ka this summer?"

"It's where the action is."

Zeke frowned, thinking, I'm getting the wrong reputation. He hadn't planned on going to Garu'ka, but the young lady was right. In archeology circles, Garu'ka was the center of attention right now. "You give me ideas, Miss Grdinich." She smiled, showing green gums, and he asked, "Does that stuff wear off or what?"

Before she could answer a silver robot pushed through the exiting crowd. "Make way, please. Thank you for your cooperation."

"Company," said Miss Grdinich.

"Dr. Bones," said the robot, "there is someone who wishes to see you most urgently."

"Show him in."

"I don't think I can do that, Doctor. He seems to have collapsed out here in the hall. A major malfunction, sir. I have alerted the medics."

For several seconds Zeke knelt over the sprawling body, feeling for a pulse. The bloodied fellow was alive, but barely. Zeke looked up into the circle of faces that pressed close. "Does anyone know who..." He stopped and examined the face again. "Carlos...my God...Carlos Janova..." They had shipped together in the Legion of Ares. How the years had changed him. "Carlos," he said, loudly.

The glazed eyes stared up at Zeke. A twisted grimace that might have been a smile of recognition appeared on Janova's sweaty, blood-smeared face. Slowly, painfully, he reached out, grabbing Zeke's hand.

"What is it, Carlos? What's happened to you?"

Janova swallowed and tried to speak. Nothing came out.

Zeke looked up and yelled at the robot. "How long has he been out here?"

"Four minutes twenty-seven seconds, now."

"Why didn't you tell me?"

"Lectures must not be interrupted for friendly visits, Doctor. That is the rule."

Zeke swore. "All right, where's that medibot?"

"On its way, Doctor." The robot swiveled and rolled forward into the crown. "Clear the hall, please. Emergency vehicles are due at any moment. Make way, please."

Zeke slipped his hand behind Janova's sopping back and pulled him into an awkward sitting position. "Take it easy, Carlos. Help is on the way."

Janova tried to speak, words forming silently on his bruised lips. Zeke bent near. "What is it, Carlos?"

"Bones . . ." he said.

"I'm here, Carlos."

"Bones . . ."

Zeke saw bright light reflected in his eyes. Shadows shifted and rotated, and a murmur went through the crowd. Zeke looked back, annoyed. Newscams floated into view, aimed at his face. "Damn it!"

"*Bones* . . ." said Carlos, his eyes wide, pupils dilated despite the glare of lights. Something flickered there, deep within his eyes: the ghost of a thought, trying to escape. It would not come —not now, not ever.

The crowd knew long before Zeke could face it. Janova was dead.

The medibot rolled forward, saying, "Make way! Make way! Emergency! Emergency! You there, get away from that man!"

"You're late," said Zeke, standing up.

The newscams dipped and fluttered. Zeke stared at one of them, noting the flimsy, ornamental wings. They meant only one thing.

Someone was clumping down the hallway, yelling, "Back off! Out of my way!"

Sylvie Pharr pushed through the crowd. Slim, dark eyes and ebony black hair—she looked like a Hollywood version of Cleopatra.

He said, "What are you doing here?"

"I want to go with you to Garu'ka."

Again Garu'ka. What the hell *was* this? "I'm not going to Garu'ka."

"Wanna bet?" She reached out, smiling, took his hand firmly —and pulled him out of the way so her newscams could zoom in on Janova's dead eyes.

His smile turned downward. "You sure haven't changed."

CHAPTER 3

The cop was real, the coroner was an android. Both had curly blond hair and looked to be ten or fifteen pounds overweight.

The plainclothes New Haven police detective was named McClennan. He made another slow circuit of the gray metal table that held the bruised, naked body of Carlos Janova. "So it's like this. You come out and find him on the floor. He says your name a couple of times: 'Zeke, Zeke.' And then he dies. Is that what you're saying?"

Zeke hesitated, then nodded. "Pretty much." He was leaning, arms folded, against the cold gray metal wall of the medical examiner's van.

"He said nothing else?"

"No."

McClennan watched the android bend to examine the body. Janova showed the old scars of his Legion days.

McClennan said, "You know he was coming?"

"No. I didn't even recognize him, at first. I haven't heard from him in five standard years."

"You served together in the Legion of Ares."

"I think we've established that."

"Isn't he kind of old?"

"When we were in the Legion, he was younger than I was."

McClennan thought about that one for a moment. "Our old friend relativity, right?"

Zeke shrugged. "My ship is fitted with invariance overdrive. It's all I ever use."

"Yeah, and I guess you can afford it—owning half of BEC the way you do."

Zeke said nothing.

McClennan took another trip around the body. The android was making a microscopic inspection of Janova's arms.

The cop said, "Okay, the man was a diplomat, right? But the

Interplanetary Diplomatic Service has already denied that he was acting in any official capacity. He was on leave, traveling as a private citizen."

"Which is exactly what they'd tell you if he was on a secret assignment."

"I know," said McClennan, "but I have to start somewhere."

"Ah," said the blond android. He drew a red circle around the inside of Janova's left arm.

"Something?" said McClennan.

"Minute puncture," said the android. He seized a chunk of gleaming hardward from a rack and fitted it down over Janova's arm. The android punched some numbers on the keyboard, then bent to look through the eyepiece. "Yep. Point of injection."

"Injection of what?"

"Poison is indicated, yes? Loss of muscle tone, motor reflexes shot, respiratory arrest . . . something in a nice synthetic curare, I should think. A bit slow, perhaps, but sure."

"How slow?"

"One to two hours, depending on heart rate and activity. The harder you fight, the faster you die. Still, it appears this fellow lived a lot longer than anyone could have expected."

"What are you saying?" asked McClennan. "He shouldn't have made it to Bones at all?"

"Correct. He pushed himself beyond all reasonable limits."

Bones looked at Janova, remembering how tough he'd been in combat.

McClennan was still curious about the drug. "Is that sort of thing available out on—what's the name of his station—Epsilon Eridani Two?"

"Garu'ka," said Zeke. "I didn't know he was stationed on Garu'ka."

McClennan smiled. "Then you don't know everything, do you, rich guy?"

The android said, "Whether or not they have the drug on Garu'ka is moot. He was injected after he arrived on Earth. No doubt during the scuffle that produced these scrapes and bruises."

"I was thinking someone could have followed him from there," said McClennan.

"Oh, I suppose," said the android, with a petulant toss of his blond curls.

The cop dropped his chin, talking into a collar mike. "Tag, this is Mac. Get me a passenger list from Janova's flight—and find out where everybody is right now. No one ships out, got it?" His collar hissed in response, and the cop smiled at Zeke. "Now we have *two* mysteries. What was he doing here, and who killed him. Any ideas?"

Zeke shrugged. "Talk to the IDS."

McClennan tried his tough guy look. "I'm here now, talking to you. What do you think? You two shipped in the Legion of Ares together. Saw ·a lot of action, right? Went all over the galaxy, tearing planets apart and all that good stuff. Did he have any enemies in the Legion? Someone who might have had it in for him?"

Zeke took a deep breath and let it out slowly. "There are always going to be feuds and little wars on board a Legion cruiser. I think the brass encourage it, to keep an edge on the fighting folk. Everybody has enemies, till the flak starts flying."

"Now we're getting somewhere," said McClennan. "You're saying it could have been some ex-Legion goon, whacked out on long festering hatred, stoked on booze, a genuine killer, right? Knows how to do it—in fact, a guy who *likes* to kill."

"Ha," said Zeke. "Guys like that don't use slow poison. They grab you in the street and tear your face off."

"How do *you* know?"

Zeke tried on *his* tough guy face and said nothing.

Someone began pounding on the door of the van. "Campus police!"

"Lord," muttered McClennan, as he yanked the door open.

"Hi!" said Sylvie Pharr, smiling and looking past the cop. "Remember me? United Comm Interplanetary?" One of her levitating cameras poked in through the door, whining faintly.

"Oh, it's you," said McClennan. "I told you, not now. When are you going to learn a little patience?"

Zeke winced, but kept his mouth shut.

Miss Pharr held her ground. "All I need is a little more information . . . and some pix of the murdered guy."

Zeke groaned.

McClennan smiled his shark smile. "How do you know it's murder?"

Sylvie's smile matched his. "It has to be murder. The viewers demand it."

Doc Bones was sitting on the floor of his office on Level Five of the underground sector of New Yale, broad back against the pock-marked concrete wall, long arms folded across his drawn-up knees. On his desk—and overflowing to the floor beside him—was a sliding stack of ungraded student papers from his three undergraduate classes. He frowned at them, shook his head, and looked at Sylvie Pharr. "The truth is, Carlos Janova *did* say something before he died."

Miss Pharr leaned forward. "What?"

Zeke hesitated. "This is off the record, Sylvie. Until I know more about it."

"Hey, have I ever betrayed a confidence?"

He just stared at her.

She said, "All right, I mean when it was really important."

"How much extra does UCI pay for a bad memory?"

"Come on, tell me. What did Janova say?"

"He said, 'bones.'"

"Your name. That's what McClennan told me. Janova lay on the floor and—wait a minute."

"Exactly," said Zeke. "McClennan thinks he said, 'Zeke, Zeke, Zeke,' and I guess I just let him go on believing that."

"But he really said, 'bones, bones, bones.' What does that mean, he was talking about real bones?"

"He might have been."

"But what bones?"

"I had no idea until McClennan told me Janova had been stationed at Garu'ka."

"Garu'ka!" said Sylvie, her eyes lighting up. "I knew it! This is great!"

"What is?"

"Not your friend dying, I don't mean *that's* great. I mean: the rumors, the revolution, the coming war on Garu'ka. This is where the action is."

"So everyone keeps telling me."

"And now your friend . . . coming from Garu'ka . . . talking about bones . . . murdered, practically right in front of you . . . don't you see? Now you *have* to go to Garu'ka."

"Do I?"

It was beginning to sound quite plausible. "I suppose I could change my summer plans . . ."

"Change 'em," said Sylvie. "We're going to Garu'ka!"

"Not necessarily," said a gruff voice from the open doorway.

It was Marty Szigmond: a bald, silver-skinned dwarf with ominous black eyes. He was hlidskji—earth stock gone haywire in the hands of robot geneticists.

Marty threw a double armful of star charts on Zeke's desk. The pile of student papers slid a little farther, and another dozen or so poured off the desktop onto Doc Bones.

"Be careful," said Zeke, pulling a paper off his lap. He read the title: "'Why Anthropology Is So Neat.' Oh, boy, I can hardly wait to read this one."

"Later," said Marty. "We're due in a conference room on Level Three in twenty minutes."

"What for?" asked Sylvie.

"You're not invited," said Marty.

"Who wants me?" asked Zeke.

"High mucky-mucks from the government. They want to talk about bones," said Marty. "Garukan bones."

"It's obvious," said Sylvie. "They want him to go to Garu'ka and look at . . ."

Marty was vigorously shaking his head. "He won't have to go to Garu'ka. The bones are on their way here."

CHAPTER 4

"I don't like it," said Doc Bones. "From what you've been telling me, Grover, the whole thing was handled wrong."

Grover Saalfield was a tall, black man in his middle fifties; a lifer in the diplomatic corps. He watched Zeke pacing the large, cream-colored university meeting room. "We crave your expertise," he said, in his deep, calm voice. "That's one of the reasons the government wants you to meet with Professor Elliot."

"When?"

"Hard to say, exactly. He's coming in by IO ship early next week."

"And he's got the bones?"

"That's what the message states."

"All of them?"

"That we know of."

Zeke shook his head. "And the Garukans let them go?"

"It wasn't their decision," said Saalfield's partner, a young man with a rather sneering expression. Bones stopped to look at him. Was this what the universities were producing these days?

Saalfield said, "The situation on Garu'ka is fast deteriorating, Dr. Bones. Control of the planet is leaving our hands. Armed insurrection seems imminent—and all my information convinces me the discovery of these fossils can only encourage the rebels to attack. If the bones had stayed on Garu'ka, they would probably have been seized and destroyed."

"I want to go there anyway," said Bones. "I have to see where the bones came from."

"Impossible," said the young diplomat.

Saalfield amended that. "What you ask is extremely difficult."

Bones had to smile. The answers were the same, only the phrasing differed. He said, "If I can't go to Garu'ka, there's

21

hardly any point in my looking at the fossils. If the situation is as hectic as you say—"

"It's worse," said the young man.

"—then everything about the bones are in doubt," said Zeke. "Archeology is like lovemaking: best performed with energy . . . and patience."

Saalfield smiled.

Bones said, "You want my cooperation, here are my terms. I have got to go to Garu'ka. That's point one. Point two is that when I go, I will not be a stooge for Earth. In my opinion, Garu'ka has every right to be free of Earth's dominion. If the rebels . . . well, I don't necessarily endorse their methods. Violence is a last resort."

Saalfield smiled again, and his partner said, "We realize your first loyalty is to scientific truth. I guess you could say you're notorious for that. And we respect it."

"And you *use* it," said Zeke.

Saalfield nodded. "No question: you enhance the government's reputation. That we would ask you to examine the fossils, suggests we also respect scientific truth."

"Do you?"

"Especially in this case," said Saalfield. "You see, we know what Professor Elliot has concluded, after studying the fossils."

Zeke didn't like the sound of that. "Don't tell me," he said. "Elliot has got himself a kind of missing link, proving that humans and Garukans sprung from a common ancestor. And that humans are the more advanced cousin of the family."

"Those are the facts," said Saalfield's companion, looking insufferably superior. "And Elliot is one of the top men in the field."

"I know Elliot," said Zeke. "He's well respected—but that doesn't mean he can't make mistakes."

"He's only been working sites on Garu'ka for ten or fifteen years."

"Oh, is that right?" said Bones. "I guess that makes me some kind of tourist, right? Listen, *pal*, I've dug a few holes in my short career."

"So what?" said the man. "We happen to have the *facts* on our side."

"Bullshit," said Zeke. "Elliot just knows fossils. What about the genetic survey? If you compare the DNA of humans and Garukans—"

"You get controversy," said the young diplomat. "The history of genetic study on Garu'ka is full of fraud and incompetence and unreliable—"

"You wanna know what *I* think?" said Bones. "The so-called provisional government on Garu'ka is afraid to—"

"*You're* the one who—"

"Gentlemen," said Saalfield, moving to defuse the tension, "these matters are not going to be settled in this room." He stepped between the men. "Are they?"

Zeke brooded for a moment, then he smiled, shaking his head. "You're right. I'll have to see the evidence."

"You will," said Saalfield. "In three or four days, at the New Peabody. Professor Elliot will show you everything."

"And then you decide," said the young government man.

"I will," said Bones. "Just make the arrangements for my trip to Garu'ka. I'll need permits for me and my crew."

The young man glared, turning to his boss in a kind of measured outrage, as if to say: Doesn't this guy listen?

"I'm serious," said Zeke.

Saalfield watched Bones for a moment, then nodded his head almost imperceptibly.

Marty Szigmond was waiting for him out in the hall, striking dwarfish he-man poses for Sylvie's cameras. The cameras looked almost as bored as Sylvie. She saw Zeke first and ran toward him.

"What's the deal, Bones? Are you still going to Garu'ka? Did they tell you you *couldn't* go? Did they say when the skeleton is coming? Did they say what the skeleton proves? What did they want to know? Are you gonna work for them, or do they want you to lay off? Come on, Zeke. Tell me *something!*"

She stopped for breath, and Marty took up the chant, asking many of the same questions until Zeke waved his arm in the air, cutting them off. "*Enough!*"

"I should have been in there," said Marty. "What, they don't trust me? Don't they realize we have no secrets from one another? I have to know everything. I have to plan. I have to make ready. I have to anticipate. I have to—"

"You have to shut up!" said Zeke.

"He's not saying anything," said Sylvie. "You notice that, Marty? He hasn't said a word! What the hell's going on here, Bones? They invoke some sort of gag order?"

"You people!" said Zeke, walking down the hallway. They tagged along, and Sylvie's cameras zoomed past, taking up a leading position, looking back, lenses glittering.

"First of all," said Zeke, "cut those cameras. If I tell you anything, it's in deep background."

Sylvie swore, none too quietly. "I got my job."

"Then go do it somewhere else," said Zeke.

"Yeah," said Marty, bringing up the rear, his short legs churning. "Go find yourself some other famous playboy archeologist to bug, why don't you?"

"Back off, Marty," said Zeke. To Sylvie he said, "You can photograph me or talk to me, take your pick."

"All right!" She spoke a few weird sounding words, and the cameras closed their lens caps and dropped to the floor.

"Not good enough," said Zeke. "They might still be listening. Send them back to my office to wait for us."

Sylvie burned, and uttered the words. The cameras lifted and meandered down the hall.

"Satisfied?"

Zeke frowned. "As if you're not still recording with some microservo stuck in your hair or something."

"You want a full body search?" she asked.

"Oh, let me!" said Marty, his black eyes lighting up.

Zeke watched her squirm for a moment, then shook his head. "Pointless," he said. "A dedicated reporter like her is probably wired from the inside."

"Still," said Marty, looking disappointed.

"Maybe next time," she said, winking. She glanced up and down the empty hallway. Classes were out and the university was quiet. "Tell me what they said, Zeke. When are the bones coming in?"

"I can't say, exactly," said Zeke. "It depends on the ship's captain and the IO engineer."

"But soon," she said, prompting.

He nodded.

Marty asked, "Are we going to Garu'ka?"

"Yeah, I guess so . . . but just barely. I don't know if they're being fractious or just cautious."

"Whatever that means," said Marty, "I'm ready."

"Me, too!" said Sylvie.

Zeke looked at them both for a moment, enjoying their excitement. He wished he felt as good. Elliot's fossils were impossible

—they *had* to be—yet the self-serving machinery of government was already in greedy motion. Bones started off toward his office, walking fast on his long legs.

Marty and Sylvie ran alongside.

"Where are you going?" asked Sylvie.

"Got work to do!"

"That's right!" said Marty. "We got one expedition to cancel, and another one to plan!"

"It's not that," said Zeke. "I have two hundred and thirty-seven student papers to correct by tomorrow night."

Marty and Sylvie slowed down and let him go. They looked at each other, and Marty whispered, "Let's get out of here before he wants us to help."

"Come along, you guys!" yelled Bones. "It ain't all glamour!"

CHAPTER 5

Professor Arthur Elliot had a slight limp, which Marty pointed out to Zeke as the old man led them down a long corridor toward his lab in the New Peabody Museum. Elliot overheard him and laughed. "You're right. I fear my own bones aren't in top form anymore. Too much stoop labor in the fields."

"Stoop labor?"

"He means at the digs," said Zeke. "Archeologists are getting down on their knees and back up again all the time. It wears you out, after a while."

"It does that," said Elliot, his old-fashioned eyeglasses flashing in the overhead lights. "And I've been at it more than fifty years—started in my teens, you know: screening dirt and washing stones. There are some things you just can't trust to a robot, unfortunately."

"All the same," said Marty, "you're looking pretty spry."

"Thank you, Mr. Szigmond. And you're looking . . ." Elliot lowered his glasses and peered down at the little mutant. ". . . as well as can be expected, I suppose."

Zeke grabbed Marty by the back of his collar to keep him from swatting the playful archeologist. Elliot turned and continued down the corridor.

There were two hard looking young men standing beside the door to Elliot's lab. They examined the ID cards of Elliot and his two visitors in great detail, paying special attention to Bones and Marty. The professor seemed embarrassed, but said nothing. He stepped up to the red ID plate on the wall and placed his palm against it. Nothing happened, and he hurriedly opened the panel to reveal the keyboard, trying again with a manual code. Over his shoulder he remarked, "I'm afraid this building still refuses to recognize my prints. I think I shall have to speak to somebody."

The guards said nothing.

The code entered and approved, the door slid open. Elliot relaxed. "Come in, please, gentlemen."

Zeke pushed Marty ahead of him, into the cool, steel-walled room. Elliot followed them inside, and the door slid shut behind him, sealing the guards outside. The laboratory was large and impersonal, full of gray metal cabinets and glass-doored shelves, most of them empty. A lab on loan, evidently. It looked more like a morgue.

Especially so, because in the middle of the room, on a shiny steel table, there were spread the dull brown bones of an ancient hominid.

"Ah," said Marty, tromping over. "The missing link, in person." He reached up to grab the distal end of a thighbone.

"Don't touch that!" yelled Bones and Elliot simultaneously.

"Damn me!" said Marty, backing up, hands held high. "You guys are a bunch of old ladies."

Elliot said, "I don't want the oils of your skin to contaminate the patina of the bones."

"Well, excuse me!" said Marty.

Elliot turned to Zeke. "You can control him, can't you? The Lord knows what kind of acids ooze from his pores."

"Marty," said Zeke.

Szigmond grinned and made another grab for the bones. This time Zeke had to restrain the old man. "He's just kidding. He won't touch them."

Marty shook his head. "Nobody can take a joke anymore."

Zeke glared at him—as much to apologize for Elliot as to warn Marty—then moved closer to the table to get a better look at the fossils. "Excellent job of cleaning, professor. You've really taken your time on them."

Professor Elliot nodded. "It's a long trip from Epsilon Eridani."

Bones leaned over the table. "A female, I think, with that pelvis. Mature. About four and a half feet tall. Broken left femur, badly mended, full of calcification. It must have hurt to walk on, so she probably limped."

"Notice the skull parts," said Elliot.

Zeke moved around to the end of the table. The skull was loosely assembled with soft plastic clips. "Big hole here, fractured. She was killed with a sharp stone. Murder?"

"No doubt," said Elliot, eyes sparkling. "A million-year-old crime."

Zeke nodded. "We'll get to the question of age later."

Elliot made a slight bow.

As Zeke leaned over the table, Elliot said, "After three seasons on this site, these bones represent the first nearly complete skeleton we've ever uncovered."

"It's in excellent shape," said Zeke.

"I think you have to agree, it goes a long way to establishing a hominid ancestor."

Zeke continued his slow circuit of the table. "Maybe."

"As you can see," said Elliot, a shade impatiently, "the incisors are short and humanlike, the jaw shallow and gently rounded."

"It's been busted," said Zeke, pointing to a fissure behind the wisdom molar. "During life, I mean. Somebody must have punched her."

Elliot wasn't paying any attention. He circled the table, pointing out features that excited him. "Notice the long fingers and fully articulated thumb. The legs are long—in proportion to the trunk—and the angle of the knee is pronounced, obviously adapted to erect posture. Just look at these marvelous hip rotators."

"The skull's more the size of *Homo sapiens*," said Bones, touching his own head for comparison. "How can it be as old as you say?"

"Different rates of evolution. On Garu'ka this skull configuration was just a rung on the ladder, leading to the current—"

Bones interrupted. "The distinctive Garukan cheek ridges are missing."

"Those ridges had a million years to develop."

"But don't you think it's quite a coincidence? I mean, this skull looks like that of a modern human."

"Well, yes, perhaps." The old man cleared his throat. "But don't stop there. Look at the rib cage."

"I see it."

"Wide, massive, the sternum thick and heavy. Less exaggerated than in modern Garukans, naturally, yet clearly more Garukan than human. This skeleton is such an obvious link between—"

"Maybe too obvious," said Zeke. He looked at Marty, who shrugged.

Elliot said, "What's that supposed to mean? Dr. Bones, if the evidence fits the theory, do you throw it out? I admit I've been looking for a link, but that doesn't mean——"

"Maybe it's time," said Zeke, "to examine the documentation on this find. The provenance, the age analysis, the raw data from your lab tests."

"Of course, Dr. Bones," said Elliot. "Naturally I was expecting that. I have everything laid out in my office."

Bones smiled. "Lead on, professor."

The office was through a door inside the lab, so they didn't have to pass the guards again. For that Zeke was mildly grateful. Those men looked dangerous, and there was no telling where their loyalties lay. If this was a hoax, it was big business.

Half an hour later Doc Bones leaned back in his chair, lowering the bundle of printout sheets and faxmemos to his lap. "One point oh four million years old. It is really quite astonishing, but what can I say? Everything seems to back up your theory, professor."

From his chair behind the wide steel desk, Elliot permitted himself a small smile. "Do I detect emphasis on the word 'seems?'"

Zeke looked down at the printouts. "Okay, more than 'seems.' I admit it. Fluorine absorption tests show that all the bones are from the same era, and as for the surrounding soil—well, you really lucked out, having that strata of volcanic ash laid down across part of the body. Easy to date, right? You got the potassium-argon test. Fission track analysis. Both giving you the right answers, both nicely corrected for conditions on Garu'ka."

"Of course," said Elliot.

"That assumes," said Zeke, "that the limestone and the hardened ash strata were undisturbed at the time of the find. And that your palynologist dated his pollen correctly, and the same with the other elements of the biostratigraphy—which, as you know, can be tricky. For instance, can you be sure the volcanic tuffs are truly bracketing the site?"

Elliot stiffened. "If you wish to repeat any of the tests that I or my staff——"

"That's not the point, professor," said Zeke. "I have little doubt as to the accuracy of the tests—as far as they go. What concerns me is the provenace of the find. The bones have been removed from their place of origin—considerably removed. Now

I understand a little of the political situation on Garu'ka—that you feared for the safety of the fossils."

Elliot nodded. "The planet is about to blow wide open."

"These bones don't exactly help the situation," said Marty. "If they're authentic—"

"They are!" said Elliot. "I stake my professional reputation on that."

"Is that all?" said Marty. "There are folks on Garu'ka ready to stake their lives on—"

"That's why," said Zeke, staring pointedly at Marty, "we're all going to be extra careful on this one. We will find the truth, believe me."

Marty frowned.

"The truth is," said Elliot, "these bones are a million years old and they demonstrate without a shadow of a doubt that Garukans evolved from a humanoid ancestor."

"Ha," said Marty.

Zeke shot him another look. "Here's what bothers me, Professor Elliot. As I understand it, you were not present when the bones were actually discovered."

"That's correct. I missed it by a day, having been called back to the capital. Dr. Darma was in charge."

"Darma?" said Zeke. "That name sounds familiar."

"He's been with me for years, now. He's current chairman of the Cultural Commission."

Zeke stood for a moment, staring into space. Darma... Darma... where had he heard that name?

"Bones?" said Marty, jerking his thick chin at Elliot.

"Darma," said Zeke. "What? Oh. Uh, did he make the discovery?"

"Not exactly," said Elliot. "Let me show you."

He touched a button on his desk and a holoservo emerged from the table top. Across the room a one-meter cube of clear plastic pushed out from the wall. The servo lit up, and the cube filled with a 3-D image of the discovery site.

Zeke leaned close. The ground was almost white with thick, powdery dust, half obscuring the undulating layers of exposed strata. In the background, dark green trees covered the horizon line, above which the sky was a brilliant blue. Three humanoids in tan tunics stood squinting into the sun. They were broad shouldered and deep chested—Garukans, obviously.

At their feet was what looked like a shallow grave, perhaps

five centimeters deep. The afternoon sun cast a golden glare over everything, etching deep shadows around the edges of the cut. Emerging from the grave, like fat brown worms, were the bones of an ancient man—apparently.

"This," said Elliot, "is just the earliest part of the dig, when they were first beginning to see what they had."

"You took this picture?" asked Zeke.

"No, unfortunately I was held up in the capital. The man with red hair is Keelor Ru. Perhaps you've heard of him? Excellent chap, a local. Oh, I suppose he drinks a bit too much, but he really knows his bones."

"Never heard of him," said Zeke. "Did you ever see the bones in the ground?"

"Uh, no, not exactly," said Elliot. "But if you look into the background of this picture, I think you'll see why."

Zeke stepped around to the side of the holocube. There were armed guards back there, facing in all directions, as if they expected an attack at any moment.

"Science gives way to politics," said Bones. "Again."

"A fact of life on Garu'ka," said Elliot. "Dr. Darma thought it was imperative to remove the find as quickly as possible, for its safekeeping. I must say, I agree. Rumors had already—"

"When did you first see the bones?"

"I'm afraid it was several weeks. You see, shortly after they were removed, the site was attacked by rebels, and we had to close it down. Apparently rumors had spread that the bones proved my theory, and—well, I am certain that if they had been left *in situ*, they would have been destroyed by now."

"And when you caught up to the bones," said Zeke, "you began your tests, is that right?"

"I had only a few days, before it was necessary to bring the remains back to Earth. I'm afraid they were not safe anywhere on the planet, and there was a Consortium ship leaving for Earth, so . . ."

"Consortium? What's that?"

"A group of local businessmen."

"I see. And what happened to Keelor Ru? Did he return with you?"

"No," said Elliot. "We couldn't find him. The last message I got from him was that he feared for his life. He has since disappeared."

"Killed?"

"I have no idea. You just have to know it's a madhouse on Garu'ka right now. And it's going to get worse. When I publish my—"

"When?"

"As soon as we've had more independent confirmation of the lab results. I have a sample kit available for you, if you would like to—"

"Thank you, professor, but I don't think—"

"We'll take it with us," said Marty.

"Of course," said Elliot.

Zeke frowned. "Well, maybe we can get some work done on the trip."

"Trip?" said Elliot.

"Madhouse or not," said Zeke. "We're going to Garu'ka."

CHAPTER 6

Sylvie Pharr sat hunched in the pilot seat of the crimson hoverjet. "Watch out, half-wit!" she said, glaring at a 'copter that was passing too close. A red light blinked on her console, and a pleasant computer-generated voice was muttering, "Pull up, veer right. Pull up, veer right." Sylvie tapped the controls, and the 'copter faded beneath them, close enough to make Zeke's eyes bulge. "Get a groundcar, dummy!" she yelled.

The hoverjet straightened up again, on the way to the airport. "Damn these people!" she said.

Zeke's stomach was throbbing. "It's so soothing."

"What is?"

"Flying with you, Sylvie. I mean, gosh, you're so calm, so relaxed, so—"

"Hey, why should I tolerate a bunch of flying half-wits, most of whom are probably tooling around tonight with expired licenses and—*watch it, geek!*" She swerved again to avoid a wallowing cargo jet that struggled into the sky.

The night was foggy and the cities and towns of Connecticut were nothing but dim, blurred patches of light three thousand feet below.

"It doesn't do any good to yell at them, you know," said Zeke. "They can't—*um!*" His gut twinged with a sharp pain. Oh, no, not now. Not the chronic stomach thing again.

"Hey, I yell for *my* benefit, not theirs," said Sylvie. "You want me to repress my emotions?"

"I just want to get to the airport in one piece. I should've taken a cab."

"Not when we have things to talk about."

Zeke groaned. Couldn't the woman leave him alone?

She said, "I just want to know what happened at Elliot's lab. You saw the bones, right? Are they genuine or not?"

Zeke hesitated. "Off the record?"

33

Sylvie turned to look at him. "I swear, I won't file a single report until we're back from Garu'ka. *If* I get an exclusive."

"Fine."

"What about the bones?"

Zeke took a deep breath. His stomach cramps were coming faster and faster now, but he knew that wouldn't last. "The bones," he said. "Given the genetic studies, the bones are not very plausible . . . but they *are* very convincing . . ."

"You mean, they're fakes?"

"I don't see how, yet I think they *have* to be. But it's not the way *I* would have done it."

"What do you mean?"

"Look, if I wanted to prove the conservative point, I'd have to show two things: that the Garukans are descended from pre-human stock, and that they are from an inferior branch. A good way to do that would be to grab an unknown sample of something authentic—*Australopithecus africanus* would be perfect—then throw in some uniquely Garukan fossils—rib bones, probably—and bury the lot in the appropriate strata—make it a bit over two million years old. And there you go: hominid, but not human. Everybody pretty much agrees that *Australopithecus* was a doomed offshoot on the way to man."

"But how do you explain how they got to Garu'ka?"

"Well, you could make the case that the Earth was visited a long time ago by third-party aliens. The shri might have done it. I don't think anybody knows how long they've been roaming the galaxy. I'm not even sure *they* know."

"But the shri—"

"Or it could have been some race long since vanished. This would have happened a couple of million years ago, remember. If it happened at all."

"And you say it didn't."

"Right."

"Could you get away with it?"

"Maybe. The problem is, real *Australopithecine* skulls are too damned rare."

"Couldn't you steal one?"

"Yeah, but they're all so well known. You'd have to fiddle with it, disguise it, and I don't think Elliot is up to desecrating the real thing."

"So what has he got?"

"His fossils are a quite confusing mix of Garukan and well-developed human—yet they are definitely over a million years old."

"Well, are they fakes, or not? Make up your mind!"

"It's hard, Sylvie! If the bones are fakes, they're damned good ones. I mean, we've really come a long way since Piltdown man."

"Professor Elliot believes they're real."

"He wants to believe it, so he does. The bones are perfect proof of his theories. And besides that, the bones are . . . perfect."

"Okay, what about more tests?"

"Probably pointless . . . but worth trying, I guess. The best thing is to inspect the discovery site, to question the workers about their methods of excavation, how they did their soil sampling, that sort of stuff. I especially want to talk to a Garukan guy named Keelor Ru."

"Is he the one who found the bones?"

"Yeah, but he's missing. He may even be dead by now."

"Murdered? Like Carlos Janova?"

"It's possible."

Sylvie grinned at him. "This story might just—"

"Look out!"

"Holy crow!"

She jerked the control stick and the hoverjet ducked out of the way as a fat green flitter zoomed right at them out of the mist. Sylvie leveled off and killed the COLLISION warning. "What, is there a bull's-eye painted on this thing?"

Doc was twisted around in his seat, feeling lightheaded. He looked up and back at the flitter. "There's nobody piloting that thing, Sylvie. It's a robot . . . and here it comes again!"

The dark green machine had banked, and was diving swiftly toward them.

"Squeazel!" said Sylvie. She kicked the stick over and put the hoverjet in a steep dive. Lights blurred below them, then resolved themselves into the landing circle atop a condominium or office building. "Hold tight, Zeke!"

"Faster!" said Bones, looking back at the pursuing craft. "Come on, it's gaining on us! Can't you go any faster?" When he turned he saw the ring of light rising to meet them. "Oh, no, I didn't mean—"

"Hang on!"

When she was less than a hundred feet from the roof top, Sylvie suddenly pulled out of her dive. The hoverjet went skidding off to the side, engines screaming, and clipped somebody's heat exhaust vent.

An instant later the green flitter hit the roof with a grinding crash and a whooping explosion that send shards of glowing metal twanging off the hoverjet's bottom.

Sylvie rose up and away, banking sharply, looking back. The roof top blazed in the mist. "I guess we better go down and see what's left, don't you think? Find out who was trying to . . . uh . . . Doc? Doc?"

Bones was slumped against his seat harness, out cold.

When he awoke Sylvie was looking down at him. "Hey, see a doctor, will ya? You're scaring me."

"Where am I?"

"VIP lounge. At the airport."

Bones half rose up. "My flight to Africa . . ."

"Left half an hour ago," said Sylvie. "I got you booked on another airline in two hours, if you think you can—"

"Hey, I'm fine."

"You passed out."

"Too many gees, I guess." He smiled. "You fly pretty hard."

Sylvie looked at him critically. "It wasn't the gees, it was that damned stomach thing."

"Small metabolic glitch," he said. "I'm used to it."

He sat up. The lounge was small and empty, as if it were his own private waiting room. Well sure, when they see you're Doc Bones and you own more than half of Bones Energy Corporation, a few strings get jerked. "I feel fine."

"You look like Death's favorite nephew."

Zeke ignored that. "Is anybody checking out that flitter?"

"Am I a reporter or what? I've been on the phone all evening, talking to cops and tech guys."

"So . . ."

"So the cops dug through the wreckage. They found the parasite control box, which had overridden the robot's programming."

"Don't tell me. It was just a standard surplus item, something anybody could buy."

"Right. Impossible to trace. How'd you know?"

"That's the way it always is."

"The flitter was hot, stolen late this afternoon. It was evidently a rush job."

"Had to be," said Zeke. "I just left Professor Elliot."

Sylvie looked eager. "You sure it's connected to the Garu'ka thing?"

"What do you think?"

"I think people are sure getting violent over a pile of old bones."

Zeke shook his head. "This is just the beginning."

CHAPTER 7

Zeke was feeling considerably better. Sitting on the veranda of the Bones family home in one of the secure sectors of east Africa, gazing out across the hazy yellow plains, he was as near to peaceful as he ever got. "I ought to spend more time here."

Jackson Charles grunted, and sipped his drink. Shiny rivulets of sweat ran down his wide, black chest.

"I don't know when I'm well off," said Zeke.

"Who does?" said Jackson.

Great dark birds were circling in the afternoon sky far above, and a faint warm breeze came drifting through the surrounding stands of acacias and fluttered the leaves of potted plants in the shadow of the sheltered porch.

Settling deeper into his rattan armchair, Zeke was on the edge of dozing off. In two days the team would assemble at Cairo spaceport, where the *Ostrom*'s winged shuttle lay, getting her final service. The plans had all been made—and Bones was enjoying the momentary calm.

He closed his eyes and listened to the distant caws of the circling vultures. After a bit he became aware of a harsh droning sound somewhere in the afternoon. The bushplane bound for Nairobi, no doubt . . . except that it was getting closer. Zeke opened one eye. Something winked in the brilliant blue sky.

"Incoming," said Jackson, who was already at the railing. Bones hadn't heard him get up.

He joined Jackson at the edge of the veranda. The droning increased, and the winking light became a reflection of sunlight off some flying craft. It was coming here.

"Codes are right," said Jackson, glancing at his tiny security screen.

"I'm not expecting anybody," said Zeke. "You?"

"Nope."

Very swiftly the silver and black hoverjet swelled out to fill the clatter of its droning engines. It nosed up and dropped into the swirling dust, not twenty meters from Zeke's gate. As the engines died and the dust settled, Zeke could see a white-haired man walking in their direction.

"Oh, God," said Jackson, fading toward the house. "It's Bart Charles."

"Your daddy?"

"Tell him I'm busy," said Jackson, from the doorway. "Tell him I'm out of town."

"Okay."

"Tell him I'm dead."

"Got it."

Zeke went down the wide veranda steps and started out to meet the man. They were ten meters apart before he realized it wasn't Charles, but someone younger who looked remarkably like him.

The white-haired man stopped at the gate as Zeke approached. "Dr. Bones, you're looking better than I expected." He was a husky fellow in his forties, with tanned skin and an imperial air that seemed borrowed. "I'm pleasantly surprised, of course." He held out his hand.

Doc ignored the offered hand. He had never met the man, but he knew all there was to know. "I take it you're representing Bart Charles. You look enough like him. What do you want here?"

The man laughed. "Zeke Bones, always one hundred percent honest, eh? What do you say? Can we get out of the sun?"

Doc didn't move away from the gate. "You won't be here long enough to get a burn."

The man chuckled as if he liked it, and smoothed his wind-mussed hair. "Mine is a simple mission, Zeke. I'd just like to—" He stopped, staring past Bones. "Is that a camera?"

Zeke looked back and saw the floating recorder Sylvie had left with him. It was taping material for a freelance documentary she hoped to sell. Scene one: the explorer at home, making preparations for the expedition.

"Just ignore it," said Bones.

The man seemed derailed. He began to stammer. "Uh, Mr. Charles sent me to . . . uh . . . to visit his son, you see? And since he works for you now, I figured—"

"No."

"Excuse me?"

Bones shook his head. "I have never understood this little

game your boss plays with Jackson. The only reason he adopted him was to use him to further his business interests. Bart knows it and Jackson knows and everybody on this side of the galaxy—"

"Wait a minute." The man straightened up, his jaw set. "Are you saying I'm not *allowed* to see him?"

"No," said Bones, "I'm not saying that. As it turns out, Jackson is in . . . Paris . . . pursuing . . . uh, interests of his own."

The man's look of exaggerated surprise almost made Zeke laugh. This visit had nothing to do with Jackson.

"Well," said the white-haired man, smiling at the camera, "I guess I had quite forgotten. You know, it's always difficult to keep track of the fellow. Paris, you say?"

Zeke smiled. Sure, why not? "Paris."

The man nodded, attempting a friendly air. "I understand you're about to ship out on another of your little adventures."

"I hardly think that interests Bart Charles."

"It's just . . . well, I mean, Garu'ka. That's a pretty dangerous place."

"So they keep telling me." Zeke looked across to the landing zone. Several armed men were lounging around in the shade of the hoverjet. "Well, so long. Too bad Jackson isn't—"

"Listen to me," said the man. "I happen to know the political situation on Garu'ka is extremely tentative. I'm sure Mr. Charles wouldn't want Jackson killed on account of some stupid mission of yours."

"Jackson is capable of deciding for himself," said Bones, his tone of voice ending the conversation. "Next time he calls, I'll tell him you stopped by. Or would you like his number in Paris?"

"I can find it," said the man. He stared at Zeke for a second, glanced at the floating camera, then turned and walked briskly toward the hoverjet. He waved his right hand in a circle, signaling: wind her up!

The guards jumped to their feet and the engines began to growl. Dust lifted lazily into the pale sky, and the white-haired man disappeared into the haze. Less then a minute later the hoverjet rose out of the dust, nosed back, and took off toward the circling birds, climbing fast.

As he watched the 'jet fly away, Doc said aloud, "Gosh, what a subtle guy."

He found Jackson in the monitor room. "That wasn't Bart Charles."

"I know," said Jackson. "I got a good look at him with Sylvie's camera."

Zeke laughed. "That thing *was* getting a little nosy."

"I thought he had a knife or something in his hand, but I couldn't catch him at it. When I got the close-up, his hand was empty."

"A creepy guy," said Zeke. "Maybe we should run the tapes over, just to be sure."

"Here's something more important," said Jackson. "While you were out there, the Garukan permits came through the fax."

"And?"

"It's bad news, boss. Only three of us are allowed on the planet at any given time. That's you, of course, and Sylvie... naturally." He smirked, but went on. "And one other. Me, Marty, or Kadak!xa, that's it."

"Damn."

"That's not all, boss. We're restricted on equipment. Two hundred kilos."

"Well, that's not too bad."

"And no weapons."

"What? In a potential warzone?" Zeke stared at him. "You're kidding."

Jackson just grinned. "I don't think they want us to go."

"Let me see," said Zeke, reaching for the faxmemos. As he read, one sheet dropped to the floor. "It's ridiculous," he said, bending over. "According to this—"

An explosion ripped through the room, a spray of jagged metal filling the space where Zeke's head had been. He hugged the floor a moment, swearing loudly, then Jackson groaned and landed on him, his hard, black chest already slick with blood.

Zeke called Sylvie from the hospital in Nairobi. "He'll be all right. Stay on schedule."

"But how could—"

"It was a rocket," said Zeke. "We actually got a blurred picture of it coming in. Your roving camera."

"But who—"

"We'll talk later, okay? On a more secure line. Suffice it to say, we'll probably never prove anything. Just stay on schedule."

"I will."

"And don't come near the hospital. He's already off the list, but you're not."

"I'm not afraid."

"No, but you don't want him finished off while they try for you, do you?"

After a pause: "I'll stay on schedule."

"Thank you," he said.

"And listen, while you're at the hospital anyway. . ."

"I'm fine, leave me alone."

"Just a thought."

He smiled at her image on the picturephone. "I know."

Zeke stopped dictating notes when the large packing crate came rolling into his workshop. It looked like a coffin on a robot dolly, and it was followed by Marty Szigmond, his silver skin glowing in the light of the desklamp. "Our worries are over."

Zeke nodded and whispered to the dictation servo, which crawled away and into its box. "Could you be more specific?"

"Whoa, dolly!" Marty told the robot. The wheels locked, and the coffin-like box slid forward, nearly tipping off the skids. "Take five." The dolly sighed pneumatically.

Doc Bones stood up and circled the crate. "I was beginning to wonder if you were going to make it."

"Last minute shopping in New Haven," said Marty, leaning on the box. "Whereby, I have solved our most pressing problem."

"Which is?"

"Staffing."

"Staffing?"

"Staffing!" said Marty. "Look, boss. We're short two members of our merry band: Reelys is hung up 'cause of that phony transport labor dispute, and Jackson . . . well, Jackson's staying home in bed."

"What's in the box?"

"And even worse, this damned restriction on permits, allowing only three of us—"

"What's in the box?"

"The answer to our prayers, boss. A crewmember we can list as equipment." He thumped the crate.

"Quiet out there!" said a voice from the box. "I'm calibrating."

Marty banged the crate again. "Shut up! You're not supposed to be activated yet."

"Leave me alone, or get me out of here."

"You better sober up, pal," said Marty, as he grabbed a crowbar. The long staples squealed and barked as they came out, and in less than a minute Marty had the lid off the crate. A copper colored, vaguely humanoid robot sat up and looked around. White kernels of plastic excelsior fell away from his rounded head like fat chunks of dandruff. "It has been a dreadful journey, and you—" the robot said, pointing at Marty, "don't look a bit more civilized than you did in the shop this morning."

"That's not your problem, metalman," said Marty. "You're here to do a job."

"I shall certainly endeavor to please you—however annoying that might be." The robot swiveled its head toward Zeke Bones. "Who are you?"

Zeke told him, an amused smile playing at the corners of his mouth. "So, what are you going to do for us?"

"Ah," said the robot. "Allow me to introduce myself. In my current mode I answer to the name of Professor Digger, expert in all manner of archeological matters. Actually, I am a general purpose robot, but with the insertion of this simple module—" Professor Digger reached into the back of his head and yanked out a small cube of black plastic. His red eyes flickered, and he held the cube up to his face. "Uh, with this cube . . . I . . . um . . . with this . . . *cube* . . ."

"Excellent," said Zeke.

Marty growled and snatched the black cube from the robot, jamming it back into the hole in its head. Again, the red eyes flickered.

"Ah," said the robot. "Allow me to introduce myself. In my current mode—"

"Professor Digger, I presume," said Zeke.

"Oh," said the robot. "You've heard of me?"

"Tell him what you can do," said Marty.

"You name it, I can do it," said the robot. "Fluent in seven hundred and forty-three languages and dialects, checked out in dozens of ground and flying vehicles, able to wash dishes and babies without breaking either, master of first aid up through elective surgery—I could do wonders with your little friend here—"

"Can it!" said Marty.

The professor continued. "And—naturally—I am an excellent ballroom dancer."

"That's nice," said Zeke. He turned to Marty. "I'm not really sure we need this fellow on our trip."

"I'm beginning to agree," said the little man.

"For one thing," said Zeke. "If he was any good, he could have *dug* his way out of that box."

CHAPTER 8

Zeke Bones was already in the *Ostrom*'s winged shuttle, running pre-flight checks, when Sylvie Pharr's taxi dropped to the wide tarmac of Cairo spaceport. Zeke's radio hissed, and Sylvie said, "Told ya I'd make it!"

Marty unstrapped. "I'll go let her in."

"Thanks."

By the time she was in the cabin, Zeke had tower clearance, and the shuttle was rolling toward the blast zone.

"Sorry, guys," she said, strapping herself in. "Somebody was following me and I didn't want to lead him here."

"I appreciate the thought," said Zeke, watching the screens for final clearance. "But it was probably pointless. If they knew you, they must have known you're about to join me on the *Ostrom* for a trip to Garu'ka, and anybody who knows me knows the *Ostrom*'s shuttle is based here at Cairo. So I don't think they'd follow you to get to me."

"Are you sure?"

"Yeah," said Marty. "He probably just wanted to kill you."

"Kill me? Are you kidding?"

"As a warning to me," said Zeke. "I said you were probably on the list."

"Yeah, but *kill* me?"

"Don't be so sensitive," said Marty.

"Sensitive? Is that what I sound like? Huh, Zeke? Am I too—"

"Hang on!" said Zeke, not wanting to get involved. The shuttle rocketed into the sky with a sickening roar.

Halfway up to orbit Sylvie said, "Hey, Bones, didn't I see you on the tube the other day, talking about the fossils from Garu'ka?"

"Ask me later, okay? I'm busy!"

45

"Yeah, but didn't you make a bunch of claims, about how the bones were fakes and all that?"

"Don't distract me!"

She persisted, despite the gees on her chest. "You said you were going to prove the bones were faked."

"I said I'd try, that's all!"

The shuttle approached max-Q, and Bones throttled down a tad, easing the dynamic load. The ship kept on accelerating.

"I just felt kind of left out," said Sylvie. "That's all."

"I got jumped by reporters, okay?" said Bones. "I ended up making a brief statement. You still have your exclusive."

"I don't see how."

Bones glanced over. She looked crushed, but then, so did they all.

"Sorry," he said.

"Sure."

Zeke located the *Ostrom*'s orbital beacon and keyed the shuttle to match trajectories. The *Ostrom* grew large in the darkness of the Earth's shadow, then Zeke took the controls for the actual docking. He was glad the ride was over.

All the way from burnout Marty had argued with Sylvie about how to deal with being followed. Marty concluded that with his razor-keen senses nobody on Earth—or off-Earth, for that matter—could follow him for more than fifteen seconds without his knowledge.

"Who'd wanna follow you?" asked Sylvie.

"Plenty of people!"

Zeke popped his harness release. "Let's just drop the subject, okay? I'm getting a headache."

Both of them stared at him in silence until Zeke said, "Do not—repeat DO NOT—worry about my health."

Simultaneously they shrugged and glanced at one another, as if they'd rehearsed a comic routine.

"Please!" said Zeke, securing his control panel. "I don't like to be fussed over."

Kadak!xa was on the bridge with Coleman, the *Ostrom*'s captain, watching the screens, making sure the shuttle was secured. She turned the upper part of her huge, caterpillar-like body and lowered the hooded carapace above the rows of compound eyes. "We're ready to leave orbit anytime you want."

"Right," said Zeke.

"It's too bad about Jackson," she said, her blue gills fluttering. "I wanted to get down there to see him, but, well, you know how it is . . ."

"Don't worry about it," said Zeke. "He understands. He's just sorry he can't join us. I think he wanted to try it anyway—you know: recuperate in the sleeptank on the way to Garu'ka."

"That's no good," said Kadak!xa. "A sleeptank is not a hospital. Funny, though. I saw that big crate Marty brought with him and I thought, oh my, that isn't—"

"It isn't," said Zeke. "Just some silly project of Marty's. Professor Digger. All in all, he adds up to just about exactly our whole equipment mass quota on Garu'ka. I hope he's worth it."

Kadak!xa nodded, her crab-like mouthparts quivering, then said, "Uh, I didn't want to bring this up, but . . . who's running security this trip?"

"I didn't want to bring it up, either," said Bones.

"Oh," she said, emitting a clatter of native clicks. "Then it's Marty."

"Yep."

"Do you think he can handle it?"

"He's had combat experience, of course, and he says he knows some people on the planet—from the old days."

"I see."

There was an uncomfortable silence. Captain Coleman stared hard at some pointless readout, trying to keep out of the conversation. Kadak!xa's carapace adjusted itself nervously. Was this discussion over?

Bones said, "And I need you on the bridge. Naturally."

"Naturally."

More silence.

"Uh," said Coleman. "We're about to . . . uh . . ."

"I know, captain." Kadak!xa turned back to the control console. Pincer-like claws moved swiftly over the panel, setting switches. A horn blared, and the ship's artificial gravity dropped to nothing.

Zeke floated away, thinking, all I need is sibling rivalry.

Everybody got settled in as the ship moved out of Earth orbit. Zeke had outfitted the *Ostrom* with everything a good field lab should have: libraries of reference materials, the latest equipment for fossil cleaning and dating, casting machines to make plastic copies, full recording facilities for logging finds, and specimen collection bins.

The mate ducked her head into Zeke's cabin. "We're all set, sir. Everything stowed for main engine start."

"Thank you."

He keyed the screen's inventory. In the holding tank right now was the sample kit of volcanic soil and fossil chips that Professor Elliot had given him. Later in the flight, when they'd come out of the sleeptanks, Zeke planned to run some tests. He just *knew* there had to be a mistake someplace.

They were still inside the moon's orbit, main engine all stoked up and running hot, when he got a call from a lab technician he knew and trusted. "Turn on your fax machine," the man said. "I'm sending you some new test results."

"What's the word?" said Zeke.

"Those bones are not one point oh four million years old."

"I knew it!"

"They're closer to one point *two* million."

"Damn it! Are you sure?"

His friend laughed. "Sometimes the truth hurts."

Doc put the radio-phone on hold and watched the fax light flicker. When it stopped he picked up the phone, said, "Thanks anyway," and hung up.

A few seconds later he had the hard copies in his hand. Everything the guy said was right. The latest radioactive potassium-argon test proved the fossils even older than Elliot had thought.

Zeke tossed the faxes on the desk in his stateroom. "Now I really *do* have a headache."

Epsilon Eridani is a pale orange star almost eleven light-years from Earth. Unlike the sun, with its Nemesis, the star has no companion black hole the *Ostrom* could use as an exit point for non-relativistic translation. They would have to pound out the light-years with the matter/antimatter engine.

Top speed over the course was a mere point six five speed of light. The time dilation was not negligible—over twenty-four percent during the coasting phase—but neither was in particularly significant. For that reason, they would be spending most of the transit time in the sleeptanks.

By the time the ship reached the orbit of Jupiter, not a creature stirred on the decks or in the cabins. On the bridge lights blinked at one another, and the air became stale and frosty, as corrosive oxygen was filtered out and replaced by nitrogen and helium. Heaters turned themselves off, and the temperature dropped below zero, where the machines operated best.

The *Ostrom* had become inhospitable, aside from the sleep-tanks—which now only supported life already drained of animation.

Automatic systems searched the heavens for pulsar beacons; new calculations were completed and adjusted for time-drift. Minute course corrections were made, and in the convoluted depths of the main engine, the work of anti-protons catalyzing hydrogen continued apace.

Years drifted past....

Eight years into the trip Professor Digger began to fidget. He rose from his storage cabinet and floated through the deserted corridors of the ship, looking for Dr. Ezekiel Bones. Professor Digger had instructions to kill the man.

Deep within his silent brain there was a knot of machine agony, as the parasite control box fought with prime directives for the leadership of the robot's body. His metal fingers clenched and unclenched wherever he went.

He entered the cryogenics bay, searching for his victim—but his sensors told him there were no life-forms there. The room was filled with the cold, unmoving shapes of the dead. If a man named Zeke Bones was in there, Professor Digger could not locate him.

The robot wandered the empty hallways and rooms and labs, nosing about in storage bins and equipment bays. When he had searched the entire ship, he went back through again. There was simply nobody there.

Professor Digger returned to his cabinet and shut down. The debate within his machine soul drifted into indecision. He would try again, later.

CHAPTER 9

The *Ostrom* was less than a month out from Epsilon Eridani's void point when revival systems began to switch on. The astrogation computers had never slept, monitoring pulsars and making tiny changes in the ship's direction. Now, as the journey neared its conclusion, and the orange star floated in the cross hairs of the deflection sight of the IO computer, the matter/antimatter engine was again pounding away, eating the momentum won through such hard work during the acceleration phase of the trip.

Doc Bones sat up and rubbed his face. He set a shaving servo loose, which mowed the stunted growth on his cheeks with a happy buzz. When the servo was finished, Bones yawned and wondered if anyone would bring him coffee if he hollered.

He didn't even have to try. "Good morning," said Professor Digger, stepping to the lip of the sleeptank. "Though I trust you detect the ironic error in my statement, it is necessary to look beyond it to the contextual data stored within. To be precise: I wish you happiness upon waking."

Zeke yawned again. "I understand."

"Kadak!xa and Captain Coleman are awake and on the bridge."

"Thank you. Is that coffee in your hand?" Steam rose lazily from the cup, which reminded Bones that the ship was still in the deceleration mode. In free-fall, steam just sat there. He smiled. "Or is that yours?"

"As you might imagine," said Professor Digger, "nutrition escapes me. This fluid is definitely for you."

"Good," said Zeke. "Let me have it."

The cup jiggled, and coffee spilled onto the saucer. "I beg your pardon," said Professor Digger.

"Not your fault," said Bones, reaching for the cup.

"Hey, Doc!" yelled Marty, sitting up in his own tank. "Did I miss breakfast?"

"Not yet," said Bones, raising the cup to his lips.

A feminine voice rang out. "Hey, where's mine?"

"Morning, Sylvie," said Zeke. He waved the cup. "Ask Digger to get you some."

She hopped from her tank. "Just a sip! Please!"

"Get your own," said Bones. "Professor? Do you mind?"

"I will get you some coffee, miss," said the robot.

"That's all right," she said. "I'll drink his."

Digger's arm shot out, holding her back. "This fluid is for Dr. Ezekiel Bones. You must not drink it."

"Hey, come on! Just a sip!" She looked back and read the data off her sleeptank's screen. "Damn, I *knew* I needed coffee. I've been zonked out for thirteen years, three months, two days, and—"

"Not a drop!" said Professor Digger. "I must insist!"

"Ah," said Zeke. "Robot loyalty—it's wonderful." He raised the cup to his lips for the second time, as everyone watched. He stopped. "Hey, what's the deal here? You gonna watch me drink the whole thing?"

"Oh, sir," said Professor Digger. "It will not be necessary for you to drink the entire contents."

Zeke lowered the cup. "I will if I want to. What's the matter with everybody today?"

He again raised the cup, and again everyone watched. He smiled. "Cut it out, I just got up. Go mess with somebody else." Nobody moved, so he said, "Professor Digger, I demand that you go out and get coffee for my friends here."

The robot hesitated. "Sir?"

"Coffee," said Bones.

"Medium sweet," said Sylvie.

"Black for me," said Marty.

"Right this minute?"

"If you don't mind," said Zeke. "What else have you got to do?"

"Well, sir . . ."

"There, you see," said Zeke. "Now off you go—there's a good chap."

Digger loitered by the door, looking back. "You will drink your coffee before it gets . . . uh . . . cold . . . won't you?"

"Promise," said Zeke.

The robot backed through the door.

Zeke looked at Marty. "Have you been messing with the machine?"

"Hey, I wash my hands of the stupid hunk of junk."

Zeke raised the coffee to his lips for the fourth time, stared at Marty and Sylvie until they turned away, grumbling, then tipped the cup. At the last moment he noticed some strange movement out of the corner of his eye. Professor Digger was peeking in from the corridor. "Hey!" said Zeke, lowering the cup. "Do what I told you!"

Digger jerked himself out of sight. Zeke could hear his heavy footsteps retreating up the hallway.

"He does need some work," said Marty. "I'll get my toolkit and see what the instruction booklet has to say."

"After breakfast," said Zeke.

"What, do you think I'm crazy?" said Marty. "Of course *after* breakfast."

Bones grinned and raised the cup. This time, no distractions. He could smell the bitter steam as the coffee lifted to his lips.

Then an alarm bleeped, and the engine cut off, dropping the ship into weightlessness. The coffee was already in motion . . . and it just kept on coming, lifting out of the cup in a pulsing brown globule that smashed Zeke in the face like a balloon full of hot water. He ducked part of it and shook off the rest, sputtering and coughing as Marty and Sylvie laughed themselves sick.

The professor appeared in the doorway, still without the coffee he'd been sent for. He looked somehow disappointed.

After breakfast, Marty grabbed his toolkit and went looking for Professor Digger. The robot was holed up in a storage room, sitting on a large red drum of thirty-weight motor oil.

"You sure made yourself scarce," said Marty, putting down his tools. Artificial gravity had been established since Doc's coffee shower.

"Get away from me," said Professor Digger, his voice flat and ominous.

"Hey," said Marty, waving a stack of printouts. "I got your manual here."

"I mean it, little man. Back off."

"Ooooh, I'm shaking!"

"You will not be permitted to examine my innermost recesses."

"Is that right?" Marty rummaged in the toolkit and pulled out a half-meter-long number three Phillips screwdriver. "Argue with this, tinhead."

The robot sighed and tried to explain. "It is simply no use. Access to my control circuits would expose certain modifications —and that would almost certainly lead to my being prevented from carrying out the actions which I simply feel compelled to accomplish."

"Like what?" asked Marty. "What kind of modifications?"

"Ah," said the robot, "that would be telling."

Digger reached out with both hands and ran a current through Marty's head. The little man dropped like a sack of jelly donuts.

"Oh, well," said Professor Digger. "Back to work."

He hopped down from his barrel and went looking for Doc Bones. No more subtle, unreliable poison. It was time to get physical.

Zeke was in his lab, running tests on Elliot's soil sample. The results of another potassium-argon count were hissing out of the printer. The computer had already compensated for the amount of argon in the air, which might have skewed the sample. The results matched the new data to within half a percent.

"Damn it . . ." muttered Bones.

He set up another test, this time using a sample that had been sealed on Garu'ka. He looked up the atmospheric argon level on that planet and entered it into the computer. Shortly the sample was glowing in the evacuated chamber. (Zeke had pipelines running to the wake of the *Ostrom*, where the vacuum was purest.) He sat back and watched the numbers flicker on the mass spectrometer, as microscopic pockets in the soil sample gave up their ancient caches of gas.

Soon the printer was hissing out the corrected numbers. If anything, this sample was even older than the others. Shot down again.

"Son of a bitch."

One last sample of volcanic ash, taken from inside the fossil skull. Zeke was preparing it for the gas chromatograph when Professor Digger sauntered into the lab.

"Where have you been?" asked Bones.

"Charging my batteries, sir. I have some heavy work to do."

"I don't care who gave you orders, I claim priority. Do you know how to prepare zircons for a fission track inspection?"

"Yes, sir. Of course. Decaying atoms of uranium in the crystal leave tracks across the faces of—"

"Yeah, yeah, right." Zeke split his last sample. "Here, clean this up and find me some good tracks."

The robot took the plastic bag and looked at it.

"Highest priority," said Zeke. "Do this before you do anything else. You understand me?"

"Absolutely."

Zeke turned away and filled the target chamber of his chromatograph analyzer. When he looked back, Professor Digger was still there, staring at the sample of volcanic dust. His leg motors were softly whining, as if the machine were not sure which way to turn.

"Do what I tell you!" said Bones, thinking, with some of these machines you need to take a firmer hand. "Right now!"

The robot backed away with a grinding noise. A small amount of smoke seeped from his leg joints.

"Stop!" said Zeke.

The robot stopped.

"Sit down!"

The robot trembled and swayed. "I cannot . . . move . . ."

"Is there a command conflict?"

"Yes . . . I mean . . . no . . ." Professor Digger dropped the dust sample on the deck. "This is very difficult, sir. Please bear with me."

He started toward Zeke with a deliberate, downright menacing tread.

Marty groaned and rolled to a sitting position in the storeroom. The screwdriver was still gripped in his hand, and he looked at it for a bewildered moment before leaping to his feet.

"Bones! Look out! It's the professor!"

CHAPTER 10

Zeke slid away from the sluggish robot. He reached out to yank the black programming cube from the back of Digger's head—and missed. The professor swiveled, his red eyes flickering, then started once more for Bones.

"This is getting serious," muttered Zeke, feeling dizzy.

He stepped back farther and closed his eyes a moment, trying to clear his head. This would not be a good time to pass out. . . .

He opened his eyes. The room spun around once on its axis, then locked in. Zeke took a deep breath. The professor was forging ahead, moving with strained determination.

"Why are you doing this?" asked Bones.

The *Ostrom*'s PA system coughed and whined, then Marty's voice rang out. "For God's sake, Bones, stay away from Professor Digger. I think he could be dangerous."

"I figured that out already," Zeke said to himself, backing up to a wall of cabinets.

The robot held its hands out front, one finger from each extended. A blue flicker of electricity crackled between them.

"Stop where you are!" Zeke commanded. "Human protection priority override. Cancel all previous orders!"

The robot muttered a string of nonsense but continued to stumble forward. More smoke puffed from its legs.

"I *mean* it," said Bones, in a sweat to remember the appropriate words. "Uh . . . sentient life protection override. Stop where you are. Shut down your motor functions. Enter your dormant state. Stand by for maintenance adjustment. Cease all movement. Cancel all previous orders. Shut down. Crash. Stop *right now*!"

The robot slowed again, its head bobbing from side to side.

"Doc!" yelled Marty, in the doorway of the lab.

"Hey, bite his foot or something!" said Zeke.

"Don't be facetious," said Marty. He came up behind the stalled robot and clamped a memory scrambler to its back. There was a brief squeal, then the machine slumped, tottering on its automatic stabilization system.

"Thanks," said Bones.

Across the room his gas chromatograph chimed, and Zeke stepped out from behind the robot. "Let's see what we got."

Marty watched him go, then shrugged and used a tool to open the robot's chest.

Bones followed the lines coming from the plotter. "Wait a minute, I know this signature!" He typed on the computer and watched as another set of chemical peaks lined up over the first, this time in red. "That's it!"

Marty pulled his head out of the robot's chest. "What's it?"

Zeke tore the printout from the machine. "When I ran the soil sample again I found traces of 2, 4, 5-trichloropheoxyacetic acid."

"Which is?"

"A herbicide. It's used to kill the grass on rural roads, stuff like that—at least it *was*. It's a teratogen—causes monstrous birth defects—so it's banned most places, has been for hundreds of years."

"But not on Garu'ka."

"Ah," said Zeke, addressing the computer keyboard. The screen filled with text. "No, not on Garu'ka."

"And you found it . . ."

". . . in the one-million-year-old soil sample given me by Professor Elliot."

"Maybe it was contaminated. Maybe they sprayed the digging site."

"I don't care if they did," said Bones. "This sample came from *inside* the skull. I'd be surprised to hear they sprayed the site *that* thoroughly."

"That's it, then," said Marty, sounding a bit deflated. "Now all you have to do is discover who manufactured the fakes."

Bones nodded, then fell silent.

"What? Something you overlooked?"

"That's it!" Zeke's hands once more flew over the computer keyboard. In moments another set of chemical peaks appeared on the screen, identical to the last.

"Damn. I'd forgotten all about this."

"Come on, give," said Marty. "Do we have proof, or don't we? What are you looking at?"

"I'm looking over, a four-leaf clover, that I overlooked before." Zeke sang slightly off-key. Marty surpressed an impulse to cover his ears.

"Amazing how song lyrics can pop into your consciousness, totally unbidden, in response to the proper stimulus."

"Sure," Marty said amiably. "But what does clover have to do with the authenticity of the fossils?"

"Plenty. The ancient flora on Garu'ka were in fierce competition for optimum environments to exploit. There was a particularly hardy type of ground-cover clover that flourished in open areas. It needed direct sunlight to thrive, and had a potent protection against the invasion of trees: it secreted a substance that attacked and withered the roots of saplings."

"Let me guess," said Marty. "It manufactured its own trichlor ... whatever ... acid."

"Go to the head of the class."

"So the substance exists—or at least existed—naturally on Garu'ka. That means that the traces you found in the skull could prove that the fossils are *real*, if the clover was part of the food chain of the ancient Garukans. Was it?"

"It could have been. I still think that what we have is a modern skull with traces of herbicide, but the case could be made either way. The bottom line is that I still haven't found the proof I'm looking for."

On the final leg of the trip to Garu'ka, Zeke and the others prepared for the landing and mapped strategy for the investigation. Finding Keelor Ru was high on the list, as was the interview with Dr. Darma. (That was a name that still sounded familiar to Doc, but he couldn't place it—and the computer had no record.)

"Don't forget Carlos Janova," said Sylvie.

"I haven't forgotten him," said Bones. "But what can I do? I'm not a homicide cop."

"You're still going to investigate, aren't you?"

"As much as I can," said Bones. "But there are other issues at stake."

"Yeah, sure, I understand." She was still miffed nobody had alerted her to the robot rebellion so she could get some of it on tape.

Marty had subsequently torn the machine apart, finding what

they all expected: another anonymous parasite control box. Whoever it was dogging their steps, he must have followed Marty into that robot shop in New Haven—or the switch could never have been made.

Sylvie didn't let the little man forget his boasts about spotting a tail. Tempers flared.

"Settle down, everybody," said Zeke. "Or I'll take Kadak!xa with me and leave you *both* on the ship."

Marty grumbled a moment, then nodded at Sylvie. She smiled back, but it was all on tape.

An alarm warbled through the galley.

"Here it comes," said Zeke, shivering.

"I hate this part," said Marty. He got a grip on the table.

Professor Digger appeared in the doorway. "Sir, the captain informs me the ship is ready for IO conversion. Where is my station?"

"It doesn't matter," said Zeke.

The ship's alarm rose in pitch, then cut off. Lights flashed, and a computer voice boomed from the PA, counting down the seconds.

At zero the ship jiggled in the violet light of the IO field. The field collapsed, squeezing the ship to the size of a singularity, then—ten to the minus one hundred seconds later—the field swelled out. The distant stars had shifted a notch, time-space having been rotated and folded back.

In the seventeen years since the *Ostrom*'s journey began, Epsilon Eridani had moved about a hundred sixty billion kilometers. At the moment before IO conversion the *Ostrom* was floating in the dark, lonely space if left behind. Now the orange glare of the target star flooded through the ports.

"Bull's-eye," muttered Zeke.

Multiple images of Garu'ka filled the screens. Blue water, white sand, green forests and prairies: the place looked fresh and unspoiled.

"Hey, Zeke," said Sylvie, pointing at the 10X screen. "What's that white bump in the middle of the forest?"

He looked up. "That's the Sacred Mound. Not far from there, to the southeast, is the dig site where Elliot got his fossils. The whole place is in the middle of what the natives call the Great Wilderness."

"That's a big rock," said Sylvie.

"Looks like it's been clobbered," said Marty.

"Yeah?" Zeke moved closer, then bumped the screen to 20X. A sizable crater, half hidden in shadow, scarred the northeast corner of the Mound. "I think that's new." He bumped the magnification again. "Looks like a lava dome in the middle."

"Volcano?" asked Sylvie.

"I don't know."

"Whatever," said Marty, already sounding bored. He spun the trackball, shifting the scope's cross hairs to the west coast, then set it scanning across the gleaming tops of a city made of marble and glass.

"It looks pretty," said Sylvie.

"More important," said Marty, "is what the guide book says about restaurants."

"Whatever they're like," said Zeke, "you won't be satisfied."

"Not from lack of sampling," said Sylvie.

"Very funny," said Marty. "Two ultra-skinny critics gang up to find fault with perfectly normal gustatorial activities."

"He's been gnawing on the dictionary again," said Sylvie.

"You should talk," said Marty. "You're the one who files reports in Basic Standard. How many different words are there, seven?"

"Eight hundred and twenty," she said. "All incomprehensible to you, I'm sure."

"Oh yeah? Well—"

"Children . . ." said Bones. "It's not too late to put you both on ice."

Marty shivered, and turned back to the screen.

Zeke sighed. The orbit was established, Kadak!xa was muttering to herself on the bridge, and the *Ostrom*'s winged shuttle was waiting. He guessed it was time to go to work.

CHAPTER 11

Sylvie walked right up to the curved plastic windows of the downside spaceport and set her cameras loose. Past the scratched surface and the wiremesh, she had a good view of the landscape beyond the fence of the compound. In the far background were rolling hills, green with forest, dotted with brightly colored cabins. In the foreground, held in check outside the tall, no doubt electrified fence, were several thousand separatist demonstrators. Even from here banners could be seen —FREE GARU'KA! and UNITED WORLDS GO HOME! The crowd seethed and waved and jogged in place in front of a line of steadfast guards. Just inside the fence armored vehicles prowled like caged tigers. Bullhorns and portable screamers belted out slogans, blunted by the distance and the thick plastic of the windows.

Marty came up beside her. "How's it look?"

"Terrific," she said. "I'm getting some great stuff. I can't wait to get down in there."

"I'm afraid that is simply not possible," said the nervous young man who sat at his desk, facing Doc Bones.

Sylvie looked over at him. "Excuse me, sir, but as a reporter—"

"You might be harmed," said the man. He grinned at Zeke, whose serious expression did not change. "You wouldn't want that, would you, sir?"

Doc said, "She pretty much does as she pleases."

"Thank you," said Sylvie. "And as for placing myself in danger, you should know I've covered all manner of riots, wars, and rebellions."

"Garu'ka has not broken out in rebellion . . . yet," the young man said, fiddling with Doc's papers. "The government has taken steps to see that the present situation does not escalate. As a consequence you'll find some rather severe press restrictions in force here on—"

"Oh, no you don't!" said Sylvie, stepping away from the window. "It's one thing to joke around about my alleged safety—but when you start talking restrictions, that's—"

"Speak to the colonel," said the young man. "He'll be here at any moment."

Bones said, "I suspect we'll be on our way before then."

"But you *must* wait," said the official, pulling Doc's papers closer to him.

Zeke sat back, looking across the desktop at his permits and traveling papers. "What are you, some kind of special customs agent?"

"Sir, I'm from the Earth consulate."

"I guess I missed that," said Zeke. "I'm a little anxious to get to work."

"I understand," said the man, looking hurt.

"I'm sorry," said Doc. "What did you say your name was?"

Now the man looked down right shocked. "Standford, sir. Stallings Standford."

Marty made a face at Sylvie, and she leaned down to whisper in his ear. Zeke had to speak up to distract the young diplomat from Marty's giggle.

"Here's the thing, Mr. Standford. I have been invited—reluctantly, I know—by the government of Garu'ka to verify some of the circumstances surrounding an archeological find."

"I know."

"Then you probably also know that I have all the permits and okays and say-so's I need to get right to work. This was all negotiated long ago. I don't *need* your permission. Nor do I need to wait for a meeting with some police colonel—that's what I presume he is."

"He is."

"We want to leave now," said Zeke. "What are you prepared to do—as a junior diplomat—to stop us?"

Stallings Standford began to take on the look of a scolded puppy dog. Doc could see the guy was trying to make points—and trying to cover his butt after getting the schedule mixed up. No doubt the colonel was to have been standing by when Zeke and his crew rolled through. "Sir," he said, "I wish you would stay . . . just for a few moments. Dr. Darma is with the colonel, and I'm sure you would like to talk to him."

"Ah, Dr. Darma," said Zeke, smiling. "You just said the magic words. I *do* want to interview Dr. Darma. But I thought he would be on site."

"He's here, in the capital," said Standford, glancing at his watch. "Right now the site is closed until Professor Elliot can—"

"Hey, Bones," said Sylvie, watching out the window. "Something you ought to see."

In the distance there were two military hoverjets approaching. "That's the colonel now," said Standford, his voice cracking with relief.

As the hoverjets crossed over the fence, a small missile burst from the crowd, riding a bright green flame. The missile glanced off the trailing 'jet, wobbled eratically, then straightened up and ploughed into the left exhaust duct of the lead ship. The ascending fireball was orange and yellow, swiftly turning black. Smoking parts shot up and out, arcing toward the concrete. A moment later the shockwave shook the plastic window, bulging it inward. The sound of the blast covered most of Standford's mumbled prayer.

Colonel Escont stood at the window with Sylvie, watching as the armored cars blasted the retreating crowd with water cannon and hard plastic shot. "You must realize," he said, smiling imperiously, "that none of your tape will be cleared."

"It's not all that dramatic, anyway—the destruction of a robot-controlled 'jet. Now, if you had been in *that* 'jet, instead of the second one . . ."

Escont glowered at Sylvie. She flashed him a wicked grin.

Doc Bones was across the room, staring at Dr. Darma. "I remember you now. Didn't you used to run a curio shop downtown? Fossils and fakes, you takes your chance."

Darma chose not to answer. His wide Garukan chest puffed out, and he looked at Standford, who said, "Dr. Darma had been the head of the Cultural Commission for several years now. I assure you the government has every confidence in his credentials."

"Whatever," said Zeke. "I just find it fascinating that a fellow who a short time ago was doctoring dog bones and calling them the ancient remains of Garukan birds should be found at ground zero on the hottest—and most controversial—archeological find in this corner of the galaxy. Don't you?"

Standford's lips silently tried out several bad replies, then he gave up and went to see if he could referee the loud argument between Sylvie and the colonel.

Dr. Darma scowled at Bones but said nothing. Zeke smiled. "Annoying to have such a squalid past, isn't it?"

Darma cleared his throat. "I'm not here to discuss the past."

"No, of course not," said Zeke. "But it's always interesting to see how the past reaches out into the present and shapes events. Being an . . . archeologist . . . I'm sure you agree."

Darma's prominent Garukan cheekbones darkened. "I do not appreciate your insinuations."

"That would be my guess, too."

Darma looked away, saying, "Nevertheless, I have been instructed by the provisional government to answer your questions. Naturally, we all want to arrive at the truth of the matter."

"Of course."

Darma looked at him. "And you've seen the data?"

"The lab tests, yes. It's the question of provenance that interests me. As you know, most of the tests date the soil the bones were found in, not the bones themselves. Naturally, I want to see the discovery site, and question every worker who might have—"

"I'm afraid you'll have some difficulty locating some of the workers. Many—well, *most* of them, actually—have scattered."

"Why?"

"Fear. Superstition. Many of the locals are quite primitive. You know, the site is in the Great Wilderness—an area sacred to them for all time."

Zeke nodded. "I am respectful of local custom."

Darma smiled. "That doesn't always matter to them."

Just before they left, Zeke took Standford aside and questioned him about Carlos Janova.

"There was no mission," said Standford, his eyes roaming. "I'm sure he was simply taking some leave time." He looked at Doc. "Naturally we were all sorry to hear he had died. Food poisoning, was it?"

"Murder."

Standford nodded. "You're right, of course. I didn't know how much you—"

"He came to see me," said Zeke. "He came to tell me something so important he couldn't use a carrier or an IO capsule ship.

He came in person to tell me something but he died before he could. Maybe . . ."

Standford's eyebrows went up.

Bones said, "Is there anything you can tell me? Anything he was working on, looking into, that sort of thing?"

Standford shook his head. "You should talk to Number One."

"I will—but I don't think it would make much difference. I get the feeling Carlos didn't trust the man. What about you? Do you trust your boss?"

Standford blustered. "Of course!"

"I guess that's a silly question," said Doc, "to ask a diplomat."

Zeke pulled Marty away from a buffet table he'd sniffed out in the next room. The little man was very busy. "Already?" he asked, whining as best he could with his mouth full.

"Duty," said Doc.

Next he pried Sylvie out of Colonel Escont's face. "We're going."

"Good," she said, backing away. "I need a shower." She turned and smiled at Zeke. "How far is the hotel?"

"Hotel?" said a stunning young redhead, who had just swept into the room. "There'll be no hotel for Doc Bones." She threw her arms around him. "He's staying at *my* place."

CHAPTER 12

Marty glanced at the immense indoor swimming pool that he was sitting beside, then out the one-way glass wall at the white and green hillside, glowing with late morning light. Next he scanned the tray of pastries resting on the table beside his lounge chair, selecting a fat, creamy eclair. He settled into a more comfortable position and murmured, "This is not half bad. I really think I was cut out for the rich life. I wonder where I went wrong?"

He took a few thoughtful bites of the eclair, contemplating the pale blue sky through the ceiling glass. Seemed a shame to have to go to work. . . .

He shoved the eclair into his mouth and picked up the picture-phone, resting it on his ample belly. He scanned the directory, found Silo's number, and keyed the automatic dialer. While the circuits did their job, he went back to work on the eclair. He was just licking the last of the goo off his fingers when the phone lit up with the picture of a wide-chested, balding Garukan. "Show yourself."

Marty grinned and flicked the privacy cover off the lens, saying, "You look half dead!"

Silo nodded without smiling. "Yeah, I'm following your example. So, it's been a long time."

"You still walking a beat?"

"Retired, Marty. It's getting rough out there."

"Lot of civil disobedience?"

"I don't know about civil. Lot of wise guys just use the excuse, you know?"

"I need to find something out. Can you help me?"

Silo shrugged. "For old time's sake."

"Guy named Carlos Janova was murdered on Earth."

"I've heard about it. A local."

"Is there any investigation on this side?"

"Not that I know of."

"Was he married?"

"I could check."

"Or a girlfriend or something. We need to talk to somebody he might have confided in."

"Who's we?"

"Doc Bones."

Silo made a face. "That wank? I've seen him on the cube. Digs up old things."

"The same. We're looking into—"

"The fossils. Yeah, I heard about them, too. Are they real?"

"Who knows? Can you help me?"

"Gimme your number. I'll get back to you."

Marty read the unlisted number off the picturephone.

"Sounds ritzy," said Silo.

"You kidding?" Marty grabbed the phone and pointed it around the room.

"Very tasty," said Silo.

"Eclairs," said Marty. "And jelly donuts, and—"

"Not that."

Marty looked beyond the tray. Sylvie had come into the room in a scandalous white bathing suit. "Gotta go!" said Marty, closing the lens cover. Silo winked out of existence. "Hey, kid," said Marty. "Join me for breakfast?"

Sylvie came over and looked at the pastries. "I don't dare."

"Pretty nice place, though—don't you think?"

She looked around—the pool, the skylight, the white enameled furniture. "It's ostentatious."

"But safer than a hotel," said Marty. "I mean, the security system here is—"

"Safety is a relative term. There are dangers that—"

"Like Merrily?"

Sylvie smiled. "Doc likes redheads, doesn't he?"

Marty shrugged.

"Every time I come into a room she's hanging on him."

"Predatory, do you think?"

"I don't want to judge the little dear."

"Doc told me about her."

"It's none of my business."

"He met her once, at his father's place in Africa."

"He meets a lot of people."

"He was twelve at the time."

Sylvie cocked her head. "Twelve?"

"And she was ten years old. Came with her father from Garu'ka. He used to be a heavyweight in diplomatic circles. Now it's mostly business." Marty glanced around the room. "I'd say he's doing all right."

"So it seems."

"Don't worry about it, kid. He's not interested."

"It's none of my business."

"She *is* awfully pretty, though," said Marty, waiting for a reaction.

Sylvie didn't answer. She just stepped to the side of the pool and dove in. Marty had to move fast to keep the splash from hitting his precious pastries.

Doc spread out another map on his bedroom floor, weighting down the corners with a green stone cat and one of his hiking boots. He leaned over the map, studying the area of the fossil find. In the center was the oval shape of the Great Wilderness, where native superstition kept travelers at a minimum. Somehow Professor Elliot had gotten permission to dig at a series of locations that began at the periphery of the forbidden zone and hopscotched closer and closer to the holiest of holies, Maru'ka Ba Nos—the Sacred Mound. It had been there, at the farthest penetration of the Great Wilderness, that the bones had been discovered. Now there was even a freshly graded dirt road leading in from the outside—the only official access. Zeke wondered how the locals were handling that incursion. Especially since the expedition had uncovered precisely the worst possible—

"Let me know if I'm bothering you," said Merrily, peeking through the open door.

"All right," said Zeke. "You're bothering me."

She grinned and skipped into the room, her flimsy negligee floating back to reveal an even skimpier nightgown. She danced around the edges of the outspread maps and dropped onto Doc's unmade bed.

"Hey, what would your father say?"

She grinned. "He's a long way from here. In fact," she said, sliding forward on her stomach, "his hunting lodge is right about . . . here." She stretched to point to a forested region on the east side of the Great Wilderness, not far from Squall City, where the new dirt road came out.

"He knows I'm here, doesn't he?" said Bones.

"Oh, sure. I talk to him almost every day. He's the one who told me you were on your way to Garu'ka."

"And he wouldn't object to . . . this?" said Doc, waving at Merrily's negligee.

She raised up and looked herself over. "I'm covered . . . pretty much."

Zeke shook his head. "Not from where I'm sitting."

Merrily slumped back into the rumpled sheets. "I'll just throw the blanket over me."

"No!"

"Are you afraid your friend might see me here?"

"Marty?"

"You know who I mean."

He did. Zeke returned to the map and tried to concentrate. He took a pencil and sketched in the contours of the crater he'd seen at the corner of the Sacred Mound.

Merrily said, "Oh, I suppose she's pretty enough. She must take treatments to get her face so smooth."

"Not that I'm aware of."

"Nice hair, if you like black."

"Uh-huh."

"Do you like black?"

"Merrily, I'm trying to get a little work done here. I know it doesn't look like it, but—"

"Are you going out there, to see where they found those old bones?"

"That's what I do now."

"Yeah, I've seen you on the cube. I used to wonder what you were like. Do you ever think about me, Zeke?"

"I barely remember you."

"You *kissed* me!"

Zeke looked up. "I was twelve years old. I kissed *every*body that year."

Merrily squirmed on the bed. "It was my first kiss."

"That's not how *I* remember it."

"I thought you said you didn't remember it at all."

"That's not what I said. I said . . . Merrily, this is not getting us anywhere. Look, I appreciate your invitation to stay at your house, but—"

"My father's house."

"Whatever. I just don't want you to think there is something between us."

Merrily pouted. "I know there isn't . . . but it's fun to specu-late."

Doc sighed. "I'm a busy guy, that's all."

"I understand."

There was a sharp knock on the door, and Zeke looked up. The door was still wide open, the way Merrily had left it, and now Sylvie stood there, mimicking Merrily's pout—and doing a pretty good job, too. "Perhaps I am disturbing . . . something."

Merrily rolled slowly off the bed. "I was just leaving."

"Don't let me chase you away," said Sylvie.

"I wouldn't dream of it," said the redhead, flowing past Doc.

When he dared to look up she was gone and Sylvie was still in the doorway, examining him. He shrugged and she left.

"Damn," he whispered. He went back to the map of the Great Wilderness, contemplating the coming serenity of battle.

CHAPTER 13

Marty was sitting in their rented car, his bald silver head barely visible over the top of the door. Black eyes blinked as Doc approached. "Still no answer?"

Zeke said, "Maybe she's in the shower or something."

"For two hours?"

Bones got behind the wheel and locked his safety belt. "I guess that would make her pretty wet by now."

"Maybe I should tell Silo. He might want to send some guys over there."

"We don't know anything's wrong." Doc started up the car. "We'll just take a run over there and see what's up."

Marty held the map out, and Doc aimed the car down the long driveway toward the steel gates.

The country around Merrily's mansion was lush and sparsely populated. There were uniformed guards at the entrance to the off-planet enclave, and powered suppressor fences around the whole thing. A very spiffy neighborhood. Past the guards, Zeke gunned the motor, headed up into the hills.

"How's Sylvie getting along?" asked Marty. "She and Red gonna be friends?"

"Not in this life."

The house was a small white cottage clinging to a wooded hill. No guards, no fence, no obvious security of any kind.

Zeke killed the motor. "Anna Serillian, right?"

"Yep."

"Did your friend say whether Carlos lived here too?"

"He didn't know. The house is in her name. Apparently Janova had an apartment in the consulate compound, but it didn't look lived in."

"Maybe we should see if we could get permission to check it out."

Marty smiled at him. "I thought you said you never wanted to talk to that guy again."

"You're right."

Zeke's interview with the number one man at the consulate had not gone especially well. On the subject of Carlos Janova, the man was sealed shut.

They got out and approached the cottage. It was constructed in frontier Garukan style—walls curved into an oval, the roof framed in timber, packed with mud, and overgrown with some sort of tough grass.

The door was more modern: steel sheathed and alarm protected. Zeke knocked, and they both listened to the silence. The nearest neighbor was a hundred meters away. Zeke tried the buzzer, but the small vidiscreen stayed blank.

"I don't hear the shower, boss," said Marty.

"Nobody home," said Zeke. "Apparently."

They went around back. The yard was overgrown with weeds and tall grass. In one corner there was a small plastic storage building, padlocked.

"I could break it," suggested Marty.

"Save your strength."

Coming around toward the front, this time on the other side of the cottage, Marty spotted the alarm box. There was a thin trickle of tarry black residue leaking out of one corner. Doc tapped the black stuff with a finger. "It's hard."

Marty pulled a long screwdriver from his pants pocket, but he couldn't reach the box. "Would you mind?" he asked Doc, handing him the screwdriver.

"Do I have to?"

"Be a man."

Zeke pried the cover off the alarm box. "Melted."

"Let me see."

Doc held Marty up to look into the box. "Melted."

Doc put him down and stepped back. "Let's call your friend."

"He's retired. He'd just tell us to call the cops."

"All right, let's call the cops."

"Don't you wanna look inside first?"

"Do you?"

"Sure," said Marty.

"Why don't you want the cops?"

"Suppose they find something bad—and smooth it over."

"A cover-up?"

"You know how Carlos came to Earth without telling anybody. He was obviously afraid of a cover-up."

"Maybe," said Zeke. "You really think the local cops are in on it?"

"Who knows?"

They went inside, past a busted window lock that somebody had put back together to look untouched. The house was empty.

"No sign of a struggle," said Marty.

"That's for sure."

Everything seemed to be in its place, though dusty. The food in the refrigerator was spoiled.

"It's been a while," said Marty, rooting about for something edible. He gave up on the refrigerator and grabbed a box of crackers from the pantry. "These are tasty," he said, his mouth full.

"Let's go," said Zeke. "Leave that here."

Marty put the box back and dusted crumbs off his shirtfront. After a moment he grabbed the box and wiped his fingerprints off with a handkerchief. "You're a witness," he told Doc, spitting bits of cracker.

Zeke waited for Marty to adjust the box so that it was in the precise spot he'd found it. The pantry was meticulously ordered. Zeke said, "Wherever she is, Anna Serillian is one hell of a fussy housekeeper."

"Don't hold that against her."

"Come on," said Zeke. "Back door."

They were on the way out when Doc saw the wooden plaque next to the door. It contained several sets of keys hung on nails beneath carefully lettered labels. "Uh-oh."

"What?" said Marty.

Hanging in the slot marked CAR/EXTRA SET was a small loop of chain containing two keys. The nail marked CAR had only a single key, and it matched neither of the car keys on the EXTRA SET chain. "This doesn't look good," said Zeke. He pulled the single key off the nail. "This is for a padlock, isn't it?"

"Looks like it."

"She's so neat," said Doc. "She would never have put it back on the wrong nail."

They both looked across the backyard to the storage hut—and the padlock that hung from the hasp.

"I hope you're wrong," said the little man.

He wasn't. The key fit.

Stallings Standford had to come down and get them out of jail. He looked awfully important and exquisitely diplomatic, shaking the hand of every detective he could reach. He reserved a small, superior smile for Doc Bones—but Doc was too wrapped up in his thoughts to pay much attention.

Two murders, so far.

This expedition was going sour, and he hadn't even properly begun.

CHAPTER 14

The next day Zeke and Marty were invited back down to police headquarters for more questions. After an hour or so, their old friend Colonel Escont came in. He nodded at the investigating detective, who stared at his notes and waited.

"So, Dr. Bones," said Escont. "Where is your lovely shadow, Miss Pharr?"

"Why?" asked Marty. "You wanna go another couple of rounds?"

"She went shopping," said Zeke.

"High fashion, eh?" said Escont.

"Guns," said Marty. "We're headed into a rather dangerous territory, you know?"

"He's kidding," said Zeke. "We understand the police will be providing an escort."

Escont smiled. "Just a token force, naturally. We don't wish to provoke the rebels. For all intents and purposes, the Great Wilderness belongs to them."

"We are a peaceful expedition," said Zeke. "We only want to learn the truth."

"The truth can be very dangerous," said the colonel.

"I can't help that," said Zeke.

Stuven La, the homicide detective looking into the murder of Anna Serillian, gathered up his papers and closed the folder. "Colonel Escont," he said, getting up.

"Are you through with them?"

"It can wait."

"Just a minute," said Bones. "I wanted to ask you some questions."

The detective hesitated. "About?"

"Missing persons."

"Not my department."

"But if the disappearance turns out to be murder?"

The fellow gazed at Zeke with new interest. "That I handle."

Doc Bones leaned back and stared at the far ceiling. "I see a middle-aged Garukan female, short, about a meter and a half, walked with a limp."

Stuven La glanced at Colonel Escont, then back to Zeke. "Mrs. R'meel."

"How long?"

"Thirty days or more."

"Who else?"

"Her roommate."

"A human female of similar age," said Bones, "bad teeth, a victim of abuse. Someone once busted her jaw."

Stuven La sat back down.

Colonel Escont wanted to know what was going on.

"I don't know yet," said Bones. "And I don't want to say anything until I know more."

"Have you seen these females?" asked Stuven La.

"I'd like to know the answer to that one myself," said Marty.

"I may have seen them," said Zeke.

"Alive?" asked Escont.

"No."

"How long had they been dead?" asked Stuven La.

"About a million years."

Despite Zeke's reluctance to get involved in a criminal investigation, he listened to the detective's preliminary report. Marty stayed outside with the colonel and talked about restaurants.

The two ladies had disappeared thirty-three days earlier. One was snatched from the apartment they shared, though there was little sign of struggle. According to witnesses, the other had never made it home that night.

"Whoever took 'em, knew 'em," said Stuven La.

"Not necessarily," said Zeke. "Not if the one on the street carried identification. Someone could have grabbed her and used her keys to get into the apartment, surprising the other."

The detective thought about that and kept quiet. Doc asked if there was anything to link them. "Did they work together?"

"No. The Garukan was a packer in a manufacturing plant. Her roommate was unemployed."

"What about medical records?" asked Bones. "If I'm right, someone had access to their files."

"What are you saying?" said Stuven La. "They were targeted deliberately?"

"They might have been. If I'm right, the kidnappers would be looking for someone with an old injury—preferably something like a badly healed broken leg. Such a detail would be convincing if one were trying to prove a primitive life."

"Primitive life? I don't follow."

"I'd rather not get more specific," said Zeke.

The detective just stared at him. "Last night you were led out of here by a Mr. Stallings Standford."

Zeke nodded.

"Dr. Bones, are you under any sort of diplomatic immunity?"

"Which I could invoke to keep you from locking me up until I decided to talk?"

Stuven La smiled.

"I don't know," said Zeke. "I'd have to ask."

"He's letting us go?" asked Marty, struggling to keep up.

"So it seems."

They were walking rapidly down the echoing halls of the police station.

"Is this the right way out?" asked Bones.

"What do you mean?"

"I mean, are we going the right way to get out of this joint?"

Marty slowed down. "Did you forget everything the Legion taught you?"

"No lectures, please."

Marty ignored him and began to point. "North, east, south, west, okay? Four exits, two of which are emergency. Alarm sounds, and everything. Side door into the parking lot—left at the last intersection, right at the end of the hall. Lots of cops use it, and there's a guard. Main entrance—down the way were going, turn right at the branching, straight on out to the street. Reception desk, vending machines, more guards. Doors are paneled in thick plastic, tinted green, and they open out. It's all perfectly obvious if you remember to look around."

Zeke smiled, giving in. "Okay, what's in the vending machines?"

Marty held up a candy bar, "Try the Nutlog. They're fresh; the guy just filled the machine."

They were at the branching. Right turn, and Zeke could see the bright green street beyond.

"Now answer my question," said Marty.

"Why wouldn't he let us go?"

"Because you sounded like you had special knowledge of a murder or two, that's why. The kind of knowledge only killers have."

"I made a deal with the guy."

"You mean you bought our way out?"

"In a manner of speaking."

They were passing the front desk and the vending machines. Zeke glanced over. The Nutlog looked superb.

"You're broke now, right?" said Marty. "We gotta hitchhike home."

"In circles of higher intelligence," said Doc, pushing on the green plastic door, "the medium of exchange is information."

"Well, la-di-da," said Marty.

"Shut up and eat your Nutlog."

CHAPTER 15

Dinner at Merrily's that night was a kind of going-away party. "Intrepid explorers, soon to embark," she said, raising her wine glass.

Marty waved his glass, black eyes wobbling with the strenuous effort to keep Merrily's robot wine steward busy. "'Trepid 'splorers!" he shouted. "Onward into a living hell! Downward into the pit of knowledge —lovely, valuable knowledge! Coin of choice for tall, skinny interlekchewals!"

Zeke nodded and smiled weakly.

"I wish I were going along," said Merrily.

"And we wish we could *take* you," said Sylvie. "Unfortunately..." Her lips dripped with artificial sweetener.

Merrily set her mouth in an expression of challenge.

Doc Bones cleared his throat. "Terrific dinner, Merrily. I especially liked the...uh...brown stuff."

"Taters!" said Marty. "Fried and refried, mixed with alligator cheese. Mmmmm! My favorite!"

"And the wine, of course," said Zeke.

"Goat wine!" said Marty. "Aged over a long afternoon and served with another mouth dribbling hunk of alligator cheese. My favorite!"

Sylvie looked at Doc and made a face. "He's had a long day," said Bones.

"He's hammered," she said.

"Garukan wine," said Merrily. "It hits everybody differently."

Zeke stood up. "Maybe I'd better get him to bed."

Marty was balancing his salad dish on his nose. "Dishes are too easy. I need something big. Where's the piano?"

"Maybe tomorrow," said Zeke, prying the little man out of his chair. His silvery skin had taken on a pinkish cast.

"Gotta go to work tomorrow," said Marty, trying to be very, very serious. "Gotta go down into the abyss of science."

"Not tomorrow," said Doc.

"The day after?"

"That's right. Bright and early."

"Am I packed yet?"

"Plenty of time."

"Am I hungry again?"

"Not until breakfast."

"Good," said Marty. "I think I'm going to be sick."

Zeke picked up the pace to the hallway. "Just let me know ahead of time, okay?"

"Sure thing, boss."

But everything was fine, and he made it to his bed without getting sick once. As Zeke tumbled him to the creaking mattress, Marty murmured, "Into the abyss, boss. Into the bottomless pit of knowledge . . . my favorite . . ."

Merrily watched her father's face form on the picturephone's screen. They smiled at one another. "I know I'm late," she asked. "We were having a party."

"Was it nice?"

"Yes and no. I wish I was going with them. It sounds like such fun."

"Well, I'm glad you're not, kitten. If what you told me yesterday is correct, the route your friends are taking leads right through the worst pockets of rebel territory. I tell you, the Great Wilderness is getting more and more dangerous. There was another rebel ultimatum today."

"You know I never watch the news. Are you sure you're safe?"

"Oh, yeah. Don't worry about me. I have my men—and I've had a new security net installed around the lodge. Everything's under control, kitten. How are things in the city?"

"Boring."

Her father smiled. "Poor baby!"

"Maybe if you weren't so rich, my life would be more interesting."

He laughed. "Don't kid yourself. Life in the real world is a bitch—you should excuse the expression."

Merrily pouted outrageously. "Are you trying to buy my happiness?"

"Why not, kitten? It's worked so far, hasn't it?"

• • •

It was after midnight when detective Stuven La called Bones. "This may interest you," Stuven said. "Although currently not employed, the human female used to work alongside her Garukan friend, so they both have medical files in the employer's private hospital."

"Who's the employer?"

Stuven La hesitated, and Zeke realized the detective wished he'd never opened the privacy cover on his picturephone lens. His face revealed too much. "There's a problem."

"What problem?" asked Bones.

"The man in question . . ."

"Man?"

"Human."

"I see."

"He's a very rich and influential citizen of Garu'ka. A member of the Consortium. I'm sure he would have nothing to do with any . . . well, with anything like what you're talking about."

"What's his name?"

Stuven looked away.

"You called to tell me," said Zeke. "Didn't you?"

Stuven La shrugged. It looked strange, something to do with the way his bones hooked up at the shoulders. Zeke was reminded again how superficial were the similarities between humans and Garukans—no matter what Professor Elliot said.

"Please," said Doc. "It could be very important."

"So long as you realize that I emphatically reject any connection between this man and . . . your business."

"I understand."

Come on, thought Zeke. Say the man's name!

"He's Warren Kingsmill."

"I see."

"I don't suppose you've ever heard of him."

"As a matter of fact, I have," said Zeke. "I'm staying in his house."

Large, black-winged insects were circling the light globes nearest the lodge. They scattered away, up into the rainy darkness, as the big chested Garukan came striding across the clearing. He stomped up the veranda steps, whipped off his broad-brimmed hat, and wiped the sweat from his forehead with a large, rough hand. He pounded on the door.

After waiting five seconds, he opened the door and walked

into the hallway of the lodge. His thick-soled hunting boots trailed mud across the gleaming yellow floorboards and onto the authentic native rugs. He smiled at that when he noticed. His grandmothers had made such rugs. Well, the natives were still working the tourists. Only now the prices were much higher.

"Hey, Kingsmill!" he yelled, standing at the wide entrance to the living room. Lots of brass and leather and oiled hardwoods. "Where the hell are you?"

"Ah, Baviera," said Kingsmill, stepping through a doorway at the far end of the large room. He had a glass in his hand, half full of ice and green fluid. "Let's get this over with."

"You ready now?" asked Baviera, gesturing at the drink.

Kingsmill ignored him. "You said there was a problem. How much is it going to cost me?"

The native hunter laughed and threw his sopping hat across the room. He dropped into a deeply cushioned couch. "You people think money is everything."

Kingsmill moved closer. "If I didn't have it, you wouldn't be here trying to get a little of it away from me."

Baviera grinned. "A little of it, that's right. The price for murder has just gone up."

Kingsmill didn't say anything.

"You hear me?" asked Baviera.

"The Rzar are merely to ambush Dr. Bones. I said nothing about murder."

"The Rzar are a peaceful people, Mr. Kingsmill. If I'm going to get them to do anything, I gotta get them whipped up pretty good. That includes the smoking of certain sacred herbs, if you get what I'm saying. By the time they hit those cars, they won't be able to do anything *but* murder."

"You're exaggerating."

Baviera smiled. Score one for Kingsmill. "Then you take care of it personally, you know them so well."

"They're your people," said Kingsmill.

"Yeah, fifty thousand years ago. I'm a lot more like you nowadays." Baviera spread his arms, gesturing at the room. "I appreciate good things now, Mr. Kingsmill. A roof that doesn't leak, a chair to sit on, a bed to sleep in. Not as soft a bed as yours, of course—I don't want to *die* in bed. But nice things, just the same. I've been learning from you, Mr. Kingsmill." Baviera propped his muddy boots on the coffee table. "I got taste now—

and it's all your fault. I simply got to have more money for this little ambush of yours."

"How much?" said Kingsmill, biting off the words.

"Twenty."

"You already agreed to fifteen."

"Yeah, I know. I'm just sick about this."

Kingsmill stood still as death for over a minute, and the only thing in the room that moved was the ice settling in his drink. Finally he said, "They're leaving in two days. They should be passing the temple the day after that. Tell the Rzar to finish the job right."

Baviera looked up at him. "Twenty thousand?"

Kingsmill nodded.

"Half tonight?"

Kingsmill nodded again, staring at his glass.

Baviera smacked his wide hands together and jumped from the couch. "Small celebration, what do you say?"

He crossed the room to the bar and snatched a full bottle from the shelf. Kingsmill said, "That's my best . . . never mind."

Baviera twisted off the cap and turned the bottle upside down in his mouth. Kingsmill was muttering something about using a glass, but Baviera was too busy swallowing. It affects the hearing, you know.

CHAPTER 16

Early that morning separatist rioters sealed off several blocks of the capital and barracaded themselves inside a number of government buildings. By the time Doc was up, some two hundred Garukans had been killed by police snipers, and many thousands injured by riot troops sweeping the streets behind armored personnel carriers and teargas rocket launchers.

He checked with Kadak!xa in the *Ostrom*. "Keep an eye on things," he said. "It's getting busy down here."

"It's busy up here, too," she said. "We got boarded."

"You're kidding. Who would—"

"The so-called government, looking for weapons."

"Bastards," said Zeke.

"Captain Coleman showed them our empty rocket bays," said Kadak!xa, "but they wanted assurances the lasers were disarmed. They took away some key firing circuits, said we'd get 'em back when we left."

"I guess there's nothing we can do about that."

"Not now there isn't."

When Zeke came in to breakfast he found Marty subdued, just poking at his grub. He still looked vaguely pink.

"Have you heard the news'?" asked Sylvie. "The Legion of Ares has two cruisers in orbit—with more on the way."

"Oh, great," said Zeke. "That's all this place needs is more provocation."

"Everybody says they're waiting for you to pronounce on the fossils."

"Me?"

"The word is, the rebels were planning a big push, but they postponed it when they heard you were coming to Garu'ka."

"Me?"

"You're famous, pal."

Doc was glum. "And I have you to thank for that."

"They say you have integrity."

"Is that right?"

"They say you're too rich to be bought off."

"Ha." He looked around the sunny breakfast room. "Have you seen Merrily this morning?"

"What happened?" asked Sylvie. "She get lost between here and your bed?"

"I sleep alone, sweetness."

Marty groaned, but apparently it was not a comment on the conversation.

"I found something out last night," said Zeke. "It may be that her father is involved in the bones."

"Really?" Sylvie's face lit up with that predatory newshound look. "Merrily, too?"

"I don't think so. She doesn't seem very interested in current affairs."

"What's Kingsmill's connection?"

"There are two people missing—a Garukan and a human—and Kingsmill had access to both their medical records. I'm trying to get a look at their x-rays."

Sylvie put down her fork. "What are you saying? That the bones are . . . fresh?"

"I told you before they look modern."

"But *fresh*?" Sylvie pushed her plate of scrambled eggs away. "You said they were well over a million years old."

"They've been aged . . . somehow."

"How?"

"I don't know. Some kind of chemical process, I guess. There's a guy in this city I want to talk to. Have you ever heard of Harden Merck?"

"I don't think so."

"He's an amateur paleontologist. About ten years ago he announced the discovery of fossil bones that were supposed to prove that certain flightless birds evolved into modern Garukans."

"I've heard that theory," she said.

"Probably because I told you," said Bones. "I also told you that I favor this theory myself. Many do. So naturally Merck's bones were big news. Unfortunately, a year or so later a closer examination revealed the bones had been artificially aged, knocked back a couple of million years. Merck was never prosecuted, but he's kept his head down ever since."

"You think he's out of retirement," said Sylvie. "You think he's the one who aged Professor Elliot's bones—so to speak."

"If anyone can do it, I'd bet on Merck. He almost got away with it last time. Maybe he's found a better process."

Marty groaned again. "Excuse me," he whispered. "Did I make a fool of myself last night?"

"Of course not," said Zeke.

Marty glowered at the breakfast that filled his plate, as yet untouched. "I could have sworn . . ."

Sylvie told Zeke, "He's been acting awfully weird lately, you notice?"

"It's the strain," said Zeke. "Taking Jackson's place and all."

She nodded, then went on about the bones. "What I don't understand, ten years ago Merck was faking the evidence in favor of the rebels—but these new bones are not helping them at all."

Doc shrugged. "Somebody got to him."

"With money?"

Doc gestured at the opulent room. "Some folks seem to like it."

Detective Stuven La provided Merck's last known address. It turned out to be the top floor of an old brick building in the crumbling heart of a warehouse district. Zeke waited for Marty to crawl out of the car. "Are you sure you're up for this?"

Marty groaned. "I feel great."

"Stay away from Garukan wine, okay? I don't think your brain chemistry can handle it."

"My brain can handle anything that pours," said the little man. The way he was walking, all bunched up, he seemed about half his usual height. Crossing the street with him was like walking a large dog.

Bones said, "It grieves me to see you in—"

"Can it!" said Marty.

The warehouse was unlocked. They trudged up three flights of stairs. By the time they reached Merck's floor, Marty was puffing loudly and spitting green phlegm.

The steel-clad door was padlocked, but the hasp was loose. Marty handed Zeke his big screwdriver and stood back.

Bones examined the enormous tool. "You know, this would make a pretty good weapon."

"That's what I thought when I brought it down here."

"Really?"

"I'm in charge of security, aren't I?"

"Of course."

Zeke hefted the screwdriver, looking at the door.

Marty said, "You never want to do anything."

"It's kinda like breaking and entering."

"We'll glue it all back together when we leave. I've got some good stuff—glue anything, anywhere."

"Yeah, but . . ."

"We're not thieves, you know."

"That's true."

"This is science."

Zeke nodded and approached the door.

"Just don't make any loud noises," said Marty. "My head is very delicate this morning."

"I'll do my best."

The screws shrieked when they pulled out, and Zeke muttered an apology as he handed the screwdriver back.

"Couldn't be helped," said Marty, his voice feeble.

They went inside. The place was full of bones. Shelf after dusty shelf: white bones, yellow bones, brown bones, bones as black as ash. Bones of animals, bones of birds, bones of giant fish. Bones still clogged with ancient mud, hard as cement, bones as clean—under a thick layer of dust—as surgical instruments.

Other shelves drooped with fat brown bottles, and the air was wet with a sharp scent of acid.

"Here's where you go," said Zeke, "when you're looking to fake some fossils. This place is a factory of fraudulent artifacts."

Marty blinked at a pile of bones. "They're not real?"

"Are you kidding? There's more bones here than in most museums. If half this stuff were real, the line of drooling paleontologists would wind ten times around the city."

Zeke reached onto a nearby shelf and selected a long brown thighbone. He blew the dust away and looked it over. Then, with a sudden motion that made Marty wince, he rapped the bone against a steel column. After examining the shattered white fibers of the broken end, he said, "Silicon polymer, soaked in a solution of iron." He sniffed the bone. "This is not even a good fake."

"It looked good to me," muttered Marty.

"An expert would not be fooled."

"You're not going to smash any more of them, are you?"

"Too loud?"

"By a wide margin."

"Sorry."

They toured the deserted room. "Some of this stuff is better than others," said Doc. "In fact, some of it is real—though not as old as it first appears. Merck is getting better and better."

"So where is he?" asked Marty. "It doesn't look like anybody's been here in months. Years, maybe."

Zeke stopped, scuffing through the dust on the floor. The only footprints in there belonged to him and Marty. "I see what you mean. Maybe they've got him in hiding somewhere. A new lab, perhaps—where he made the bones Keelor Ru found."

"He couldn't have done it here?"

Zeke looked at the ranks of chemical bottles, their labels stained and cracked. Potassium dichromate, one of them said. He smiled. That was the same brown stain Dawson had used on the Piltdown fossils. "I don't think there's anything in here he could have used. And none of these bones look even close to as good as Elliot's."

They moved out of the large room and into Merck's adjoining apartment. There was a steel door leading out to a rusted staircase. The door was locked from the inside.

A small, corroded kitchenette filled a corner of the apartment, its sink filled with crusty dishes. "I think there's something moving in there," said Marty.

One wall was loaded with books, and Zeke stepped over to look at titles. "He's got most of the classic literature—in paleoanthropology, I mean. These books could be valuable."

"Not to me," said Marty, nosing about for a place to sit down. "Look at this," he said, throwing a dusty blanket off an easy chair. "He even has bones in the living room. Talk about dedication . . ."

Zeke came up to the chair and looked. "Oh, hell . . ."

"What?"

"That could be Harden Merck himself."

Marty groaned. "I was going to *sit* there."

The skeleton was covered in leathery muck, chunks of white showing through.

"I guess we better not touch anything," said Zeke.

"I don't know about you," said Marty, "but I hadn't planned on touching anything."

CHAPTER 17

Marty yawned as he made his way through the midmorning mist. From across the city there came the intermittent rattle of gunfire, and the hiss of energy weapons, followed by the growl of power generators making up the depleted charge. Marty yawned again. It was a fine day to begin their adventure.

He found Zeke at the foot of the gently sloping front lawn, inspecting the vehicles. There were three of them, squatting on thick tires like top-heavy turtles. "We supposed to sleep in these things?" asked Marty.

"That's the idea," said Zeke, kicking a tire.

"Bitchin'."

Zeke examined him. "How do you feel?"

The little man groaned. "I'm fine. But I don't remember a thing about the party last night."

"The party was two nights ago."

"In that case I don't remember yesterday, either. But I woke up dreaming about bones."

"You should have. We found Harden Merck in his boneyard yesterday. According to Stuven La he'd been dead a year and half. I guess he doesn't get many visitors."

Marty tilted his head. "Harden Merck. Was he important?"

"Well . . . I *had* hoped he was the one who faked the fossils. I guess he wasn't. Unless they faked him, too."

Marty frowned. "This is getting too complicated."

"I agree. Have you seen Sylvie?"

"Still packing."

Zeke checked his watch, then looked out through the steel gate, where a cameraman and a reporter waited. "We were supposed to get some cops for an escort. They're late."

"We don't need 'em."

"And another thing: I arranged to take with us two local geologists, but now it seems there's some hang-up with their permits. The government is still scared I might find something out."

Marty yawned again. "Is that why we got three trucks?"

"Yeah, and we're gonna take 'em all. Things might work out yet."

Professor Digger clumped his way down the grassy hill, carrying a big suitcase. "Miss Pharr will be here shortly."

"Can you drive this vehicle?" asked Zeke.

The robot looked it over, then peered through the open window at the controls. "I feel every confidence."

"Okay, take the first one. Don't touch the radio frequency— I've already set them all to 122.655."

"I understand."

"Get inside and test the engine. We should be leaving in five minutes."

Professor Digger offered a pathetic salute and shambled off to climb into the first vehicle.

Zeke looked up the hill. Sylvie was coming, flanked by floating cameras. "Smile," he told Marty.

"I'm sick of this already."

One of the cameras peeled off to circle the vans. It stopped to focus on Professor Digger, who was studiously revving the engine and running the power windows up and down.

The other one went down by the gate to stare into the lens of the local newscamera. Sylvie shaded her eyes from the morning glare. "What does *she* want?"

"What they *all* want," said Bones. "A statement."

Sylvie looked sharply at him. "You didn't talk to her, did you?"

"Not yet, but we're going out that way. I'll have to say *some-thing*."

"Try, 'no comment.' It really makes 'em mad. Trust me."

"Yeah, yeah."

Sylvie looked the vans over. "Are we ready?"

"There's supposed to be an armed escort," said Zeke.

"Are they going all the way?"

"Well, through the city—that was the idea. Longer if needed. But they're not here yet."

"You think they're coming?"

"I don't know. I got the horrible feeling I might have to call Colonel Escont."

Sylvie grinned.

"Yeah, I know," he said. "I'm better at digging up bones."

Sylvie looked around. "Where's little Merrily?"

"I haven't seen her since last night," said Zeke.

"I saw her at breakfast," said Marty. "She said she was going into town."

"Born to shop," said Sylvie.

"She take all the guards with her?" asked Zeke.

"Beats me," said Marty.

Sylvie half closed her eyes. "Really, Zeke, you don't need guards as long as she's not around."

He nodded without comment. This mock jealousy thing was growing thin.

They waited another fifteen minutes for the police escort, but nobody showed up. "The hell with it," said Zeke. "Let's roll."

"Don't you want to call Escont?" asked Sylvie.

"Screw Escont," said Zeke. "I'm tired of dealing with guys I don't like."

They piled into the three vans and creeped down the hill to the street. Professor Digger synthesized the electronic code, and the gates swung apart. The reporter and her cameraman trotted forward, let Digger pass after some amused scrutiny, and pounced on Zeke's van.

Bones leaned out and said, "Sorry. I have no news."

Beside him Sylvie muttered, "Right."

But the reporter surprised Bones. She had news for him.

For a moment he sat stunned, as Marty honked from the van behind him. Bones was annoyed the reporter had locked onto his suspicions about the missing women, and astounded she had managed to get hold of the x-rays Stuven La had promised to locate. But that was nothing: she had compared the x-rays with photographs of Elliot's fossils. They matched.

"Tell us what this means" asked the reporter.

Bones said, "Well, I guess . . . uh . . . *ow*! Stop that!"

"Tell her, 'No comment,'" said Sylvie, jabbing him again in the ribs with her elbow. "Remember?"

The reporter persisted. "Doesn't this prove that the bones were faked?"

Zeke dropped his right arm to protect himself from Sylvie. "Look," he told the reporter, "you already know I hope to prove the bones a fake. And I will, somehow. This new information just makes me more confident, that's all."

"But the x-rays are a perfect match, Dr. Bones. How can you say—"

"No comment," Sylvie told her, leaning across Bones. "Watch for my report, honey—when this matter is settled. So long, bye-bye!"

Her foot jammed the accelerator, and Bones had to ride the brake to keep from running over the cameraman. Marty's van zoomed through the already closing gates, right behind him. When Bones looked back, the reporter was standing by the gates, making a summary statement for the camera.

"Vultures," muttered Sylvie.

"You're the expert."

"Ha ha."

The three-vehicle convoy split the iron gates of the exclusive compound and hit the road—Digger in front, Zeke and Sylvie in the middle, and Marty in the rear. Doc put his map on the re-peater, tracing the route through town for the professor. "Very well," said the robot, his voice sounding incredibly remote on the radio.

"And outside the city?" asked Sylvie.

"We have several choices," said Doc. "The access road is on the far side of the Wilderness, and we were supposed to approach it from the south. If we do, there's several ways to go, depending on the quality of the roads, and so forth. Or we could go around the forbidden zone on the north side."

"That's the long way."

"But unexpected."

"Is someone expecting us?"

Zeke remained silent for a moment, and Sylvie laughed. "You're keeping the good part to yourself."

"I already told you. Warren Kingsmill may be involved—and he knows our route."

"Merrily told him?"

"He asked her and she saw no reason not to tell him."

"You asked her?"

"Last night."

"I get it."

"In the kitchen."

"Kinky."

"Stop it."

"So okay, because he knows, you want to change the route.

Another way south . . . or all the way around the north?"

"I was also thinking of going right through the middle."

"I thought the Great Wilderness was sacred."

"There are trails. I checked. It seems the natives patrol the area—but infrequently."

"What if they catch us?"

"We'll stop and talk."

"Do you know the language?"

"I bought a data cube for Digger. He says there are no glitches."

"But he didn't test it on a native."

"Hey, it's got a money-back guarantee."

"Perfect."

There were roadblocks on the way out of town, but the police had everything in control. They looked at Doc's permits and smiled and waved him through. At one place the guard in charge halted everything to make a phone call. Doc didn't ask him who he was calling. If it was Colonel Escont, the word that came back was: let 'em pass. Then again, maybe the guy just had a sudden itch to call home and see what was on deck for supper.

When you're running risks, your imagination just keeps cranking out the horrors.

CHAPTER 18

They were on the southern route, running east, parallel to the bottom of the Great Wilderness. The road was wide and well maintained, but traffic was sparse. According to broadcasts on commercial radio, the rebellion was about to start.

"They always exaggerate," said Marty, his voice crackling with static.

Zeke keyed his radio. "Let's hope so." He hung the mike on the hook.

Sylvie turned to face him. "Do you think it really is close?"

"You getting nervous?"

"I just want to be in the right place at the right time. I'm a reporter, remember?"

"Am I boring you? What we're doing is pretty interesting."

She glanced out the window. "There's not much to see—and it's pretty clear nothing is going on."

"Something's going on. We're being tracked."

"By whom?"

Zeke pointed skyward. "You think they can't see us from orbit? On this highway we must look like perfect targets. You ever see a neutral-particle beam punch through a planet's atmosphere? It's like the biggest bolt of—"

"Then why are we—"

"Right now I want them to feel confident."

"What about the way *I* feel?" said Sylvie, looking up at the fragile ceiling of the cab.

"I thought you wanted action."

"What I want is something to aim my cameras at. Being a target in somebody's cross hairs is hard to photograph."

A cop car whizzed past, ignoring their convoy. "Lot of them on the road today," said Zeke.

"I don't mind."

"They're probably watching us too."

"Are you kidding me?"

"What do you think happened to our armed escort?"

"You mean the cops are in on the conspiracy? I don't believe it."

Doc shrugged. "Somebody is jerking some pretty heavy strings. I don't think it would be a good idea to trust anybody right now."

"Well, that's just great."

Sylvie fell silent, looking out the window. The highway cut through low, brush-covered hills. Patches of bare dirt showed white through the green.

Zeke watched the road, keeping an eye on the lead car. So far, so good.

Not long after that the news reported that Dr. Ezekiel Bones, noted archeologist from Earth, had solved the mystery of the fossil bones. Absolute fakes, he claimed, constructed from the bodies of two missing citizens.

Sylvie emitted a small shriek. "You never said that!"

Bones shushed her.

According to the report, Dr. Bones declined to say who was behind it all, but he was still investigating, and expected to have that information soon.

"Oh, sure," said Sylvie.

Next, a government spokesman came on the radio and denied the allegation, calling Dr. Bones's story preposterous. He reminded everyone of the doctor's well-publicized bias in this matter. Furthermore, he said, the government was considering a suggestion to revoke Dr. Bones's permits and visas.

"They have got to be kidding," said Sylvie.

"Don't worry about it," said Bones. "Pure harassment."

"But they have that power, don't they?"

"They've got lots of power. So what?"

Sylvie stared up at the ceiling of the cab. "I keep thinking about those particle-beam cannon."

"They're not going to hurt us," said Bones. "Not yet."

After another monotonous hour of highway driving, Zeke and Sylvie had exhausted their fund of stupid conversation. Bones didn't mind the silence. He needed time to think about Elliot's fossils. Here he was, going to the dig site to see what the place looked like, to collect soil samples of his own to test, when what he really needed was a way to test the age of the bones themselves.

The potassium-argon test worked only on volcanic tuff, which to be useful must bracket the strata where the bones were found. Same with the fission track test. The fluorine absorption test *did* examine the bones, but it was generally only used to tell the relative ages of bones found in the same area. It was difficult to calibrate for absolute age, keyed as it was to the fluorine content of specific soils. And it was easy to fake.

What Zeke needed was a test for the bones than no one could have anticipated, something they weren't likely to fake, something nobody had ever tested before.

The highway ran smoothly east, and Bones watched Digger's van as it hunkered down over the precise middle of the lane. Sylvie seemed to be dozing.

A test for the bones, thought Zeke. Something new. Something outrageous, even. It didn't have to be accurate: it just had to distinguish between modern bones and those a million or so years old.

Something weird . . . something off the wall . . . something . . . *some*thing . . .

Late in the afternoon Marty started getting cranky. He said he was tired of talking to himself all day. Besides, he'd run out of sandwiches and potato chips.

"Hang on, buddy," said Zeke. "We're stopping for the night soon."

"We better!"

They were two-thirds of the way to Squall City, gateway to the Great Wilderness. It was here the dirt road entered the forbidden zone and ran straight as it could through the mountains, past several crumbling, overgrown stone temples, to the site of the fossil find.

Sylvie was looking at the map on the repeater screen. "We could still cover more ground today."

"Won't be necessary," said Zeke. "We have an early start in the morning."

He radioed Digger and told him of the crossroads ten klicks farther on. "There's a motel complex at the second exit. We'll stay the night there and recharge the vans."

"Very well," said the professor.

Sylvie asked Zeke, "Hey, didn't you say we'd be living in the vans?"

"Take comfort when you can, Sylvie. It's going to get rough."

Sylvie didn't answer. A big black police cruiser zoomed up at them from behind and passed the convoy in a hurry, its shockwave rocking the vans. Marty was swearing on the radio, until Zeke shut him up. Professor Digger's van recovered the quickest, adjusting with precise steering corrections. The police cruiser faded into the dimming highway.

"Who the hell do they think they are?" asked Sylvie.

Zeke kept quiet. He was wondering how many cops were corrupt on this planet. And then he thought: it only takes one, if he's got the power to direct the others. . . .

Colonel Escont's practiced sneer came to mind and wouldn't go away.

The motel was rather primitive, but there was a good restaurant across the road. At least Marty pronounced it good. The portions were *huge*.

After dinner they got together in one of their two rooms and held a strategy meeting.

"We're splitting up tomorrow," said Zeke.

Marty nodded. "I was wondering when you'd get around to that."

Zeke opened the map printout. "Behind the motel is a country road that leads to the border of the Great Wilderness. There's a pass through the hills . . . right here . . . and after that there are any number of trails and dirt roads crisscrossing the forbidden zone."

"Patrolled," said Marty.

"Informally," said Doc. "And the natives are busy supporting the coming rebellion. They'll be more interested in attacking the government that in defending the Wilderness."

"But it's holy ground," said Sylvie. "Why aren't they going to defend it?"

"What are gods for?" asked Zeke. "Besides, from what I've heard, the only really sensitive spot in the whole place is Maru'ka Ba Nos, the Sacred Mound. And I hope to stay well south of that."

"Who goes where?" asked Marty.

"The three of us take two vans and cross into the zone. Professor Digger will take his van along the original route—on the highway to Squall City, then up the big dirt road to the site. Of course I don't expect him to make it that far."

"An ambush?" said Sylvie.

"Almost certainly," said Zeke. "We'll keep an eye on Digger —and see how much fire he draws."

Now the robot spoke up. "I do hope I will not sustain damage."

"When they see you're alone, they'll probably just dump you out and go looking for us. And by that time we'll be set."

"Very well, sir," said Digger. Zeke sent him outside to watch the vans.

"Personally," said Marty, "I don't think he's going to make it through this."

"What is that?" asked Zeke. "A pre-battle premonition?"

Marty shrugged. "A guy gets a feeling, sometimes."

"That's so silly," said Sylvie. "Macho combat nonsense."

"Still," said Marty. "I wouldn't want to be clanking around in *his* feet."

Later that night Bones went outside to point one of the van's big comm attennas at the *Ostrom* when she came around on her orbit. "Here's the thing, Kadak!xa. I've been trying to think of an off-the-wall way to test the age of the bones. What do you think of neutrino absorption?"

Kadak!xa laughed, a series of rather ominous clicks. "Well, it has a long baseline, that's for sure. You're thinking of the calcium, I assume."

"Right. Bones are full of calcium phosphate and calcium carbonate. What if a neutron in a calcium nucleus were hit by a neutrino?"

"The neutron would probably eject an electron and turn into a proton."

"Which means the nucleus goes up a notch to . . . uh . . . what? Help me out."

"Scandium," said Kadak!xa.

"Right. Calcium-40 to scandium-40."

"No such isotope as scandium-40," said Kadak!xa.

"Play along, okay? This stuff would probably be unstable, so—"

"Extremely unstable. It would decay into calcium-40 almost immediately. That doesn't help."

"Okay, what about calcium-44? It's the next most abundant stable isotope of calcium. If it got clobbered by a neutrino, we'd get scandium-44."

"No such isotope."

"Come on!"

"I've got it right here on the screen, Zeke. There's scandium-45 and that's it. No other isotopes."

"Good. Then what would a sample of scandium-44 do? It'd decay pretty fast, right?"

"Back into calcium-44, probably."

"Yeah, by positive beta decay. But what if it alpha-decayed?

You'd get potassium-40, which we all know decays into argon-40 —it's the same stuff we test when we run the volcanic samples."

"You can't test for argon-40 in a bone sample," said Kadak!xa. "There are no crystals to hold it in."

"I know that," said Zeke. "What I'm saying is, the sample would have an elevated amount of potassium-40. We could check for that."

"Maybe."

"We might get ballpark figures."

"There's not much bone to work with," said Kadak!xa. "And this whole thing hinges on neutrino absorption, which is not the most reliable reaction in the universe."

"Okay, I have another idea."

"You need to get some sleep."

"Listen," said Zeke. "What if the bombarding neutrinos came from stellar explosions, from supernovas? We'd still go from calcium-44 to scandium-44, but if the neutrino were energetic enough, the nucleus might be so pumped up it would eject a neutron. Then the scandium-43 would kick a positron and give us calcium-43, which is pretty rare."

"Fifth of all stable calcium isotopes," said Kadak!xa. "That might work. But we need a good reading on galactic supernovas."

"Right."

"This is not a standard test."

"That's the point."

"I'll think about it."

"Fine, think about it," said Zeke. "Then run the test, okay? I need to get some numbers."

"We'll see. Get some sleep."

"I'll try."

Zeke went back to the room, but he was too pumped up himself to sleep, as if his brain were being bombarded by billions of neutrinos every second—which, of course, it was. . . .

CHAPTER 19

Standing by the window Keelor Ru cautiously parted the dusty drapes and peered out into the dark street below. There was someone in the mouth of the cobblestoned alley across the way, a vague dark figure that seemed to be staring up at him through the warm mist.

Keelor Ru forced himself to remain rigid, and only after several long moments did he ease the curtain back and step away from the window. In the darkness of his room he felt safer. In the head pounding misery of his hangover, he found a kind of numb tranquility. If he concentrated, he might be able to forget the man in the alley.

But he couldn't concentrate.

He kept thinking they found me . . . they found me . . . they found me . . .

He backed up until he reached the far wall. There was a sound in the hall, just outside his door. He closed his eyes. The floorboards creaked, the wall thumped loudly, then a drunk began to curse. Keys jingled and scraped at the lock, and the door banged open. Keelor Ru almost screamed—

But his door was still shut. Across the hall a door slammed. There was another heavy crash, like a drunk landing face first across a rickety bed.

Keelor Ru tried to catch his breath. He wanted to go back to the window and see if the man had moved, but he was afraid. He was afraid of blundering against the curtains, afraid of being seen. And he was afraid the man would be gone.

Because men like that don't just wander away. If they moved, they moved with a purpose. If that man left the alley, it would be to come here to the room. And it would be bad for Keelor Ru to be in the room when that happened. So if he saw that the man was gone from the alley, he knew he'd have to get out of the room fast. And that was impossible. He was stuck where he was, leaned back against the wall, heart pounding hard and missing beats. All he could do was listen to the noises in the hall . . . and wait for the door to burst open.

In the distance he heard several large explosions. The windows rattled, and someone down the hall cursed drunkenly. Ru waited. Minutes later, there were sirens.

The rebels were busy tonight, blowing off bombs. It was funny. The whole damned planet was getting ready to explode, and Keelor Ru was hiding out—afraid to move. *Unable* to move.

A trickle of sweat ran down his neck. The room was hot, the air rancid, but he kept the windows shut. He deserved to suffer for his cowardice.

When he closed his eyes he could see the brow of the skull emerging from beneath the moving bristles of his brush.

The bones, the goddamn bones. He wished he'd never found them, but he had. He wished he'd just taken the money they offered and kept quiet, but he hadn't. He wished—how he wished, now—he hadn't double-crossed those gangsters and stolen the bones from Darma. But he had, he had, in a glorious, drunken state of patriotic righteousness he'd done it, he'd blown his useless life to hell.

He was an idiot, a congealed mass of misguided heroic nonsense. He was a coward and a traitor who could never be redeemed. He was worthless.

And he was stuck in this hot room, paralyzed with fear, waiting to die. Once he'd had plans, but that was all over now. Dr. Bones had been on the planet for days, but Keelor Ru was not about to leave this room. He'd paid a lot of money for a getaway car, but now he knew he'd never use it. They were out there. They had *found* him. When they decided the time was right, they'd come in here and kill him.

He curled over, hugging his knees on the dusty floor. Outside in the hall the floorboards creaked again. Keelor Ru hugged his knees and waited to die.

Zeke came off the bed in a hurry as the door opened. "Hey!" said Sylvie, eyes wide. "Take it easy. It's only me."

"Sorry."

She looked around. "You watching the cube?"

"Yeah."

"Where's Marty?"

"Looking for a snack. What's the matter, can't you sleep?"

"Haven't tried, yet. Had to clean my cameras and start 'em charging."

"The dedicated little professional, eh?"

"Don't laugh." She crossed in front of the flat video screen and sat in a stuffed chair. "What's on?"

"Local news, babe. I want to see what the weather's gonna be like."

Sylvie watched for a moment, her head cranked around at a weird angle. On the screen a bunch of soldiers fired plastic bullets at half-seen figures lurking at the end of a rubble strewn street. "Boy," she said, "that doesn't change much."

"Only for the worse, babe."

She turned from the screen and settled back in the chair. "There's one in my room just like this one."

"Volume buying, babe. That's the way it works."

"Hey, what's all this 'babe' stuff? I tell you, the closer you come to getting shot at, the more sexist you get."

"Sorry. I guess it's in the genes."

"No, it isn't."

Doc sighed and sat down on his bed. "You're right."

Sylvie stretched out and crossed her ankles. "Bet you wish Merrily were here."

"Not me."

She smiled. "You want us both?"

"Lady, I don't think I could handle either one of you."

Sylvie nodded and looked around the room. Neither said a word for several minutes. The news droned on.

Finally Zeke yawned. "Much as I value your scintillating company. . ."

"Why don't I go to bed, right?"

"We're starting before light, tomorrow."

"I remember. I just wanted to ask you something."

"Go ahead."

"What exactly are you trying to do here?"

"I'm trying to find out the truth."

"Yeah, but what if that truth leads to bloodshed?"

Bones hesitated. He remembered what Escont had told him in the police station. The truth can be dangerous.

"I know it's hard," said Zeke. "But you can't stop looking for the truth just because it might start a war."

"Don't you care?"

"Of course I care. Hey, lady, I was in the Legion of Ares for years. I saw some stuff that would . . . well, let's just say I know how bad wars can get. I know that better than you, even."

"Maybe yes, maybe no. My point is, you don't seem to want to do anything to—"

"My job is to find the truth—the scientific truth. The rest of the universe flows on past. I can't do much about it—and neither can you. But let me tell you something, when the truth is buried, the universe suffers for it, and that includes the people—*especially* the people."

She was smiling at him.

Zeke sighed. "Pardon me, was I lecturing?"

Marty came in, loaded down with bounty culled from the vending machines outside the manager's cabin. He glanced at Sylvie's relaxed posture, and at Zeke sitting so horribly upright at the foot of the bed. "Oh," he said, "did I miss a change in room assignments?"

"I'm just visiting," said Sylvie.

"I'm all for visitation rights," said Marty. "Should I come back later? I could eat this junk in the van."

"Just get in here and close the door," said Zeke. "She's on her way out, I'm sure."

Sylvie yawned and stretched, pointing her toes. "I guess he's right. Early morning, right?"

"We'll wake you," said Marty.

"Don't bother. I'll set the alarm on Professor Digger."

"You're sleeping with him tonight?" asked Marty. He looked at Doc with mock sympathy. "Sorry, boss."

Zeke said, "Tell Digger to patrol the parking lot, at random. He can stay in one of the vans—or in your room, if you prefer—the rest of the time. That'll keep him out of the mist."

"Don't want him to rust," said Marty. "Give him a good work out, okay?" He winked.

Sylvie paused at the door. "You guys deserve each other."

Late that night the mist dried out, and the stars burned brightly. A swarm of black, buzzing insects bopped their wings and circled the floodlight in front of the manager's cabin. Far overhead, moving slowly between the stars, other lights—faint and silent and ominous lights—prowled the night sky.

Professor Digger shuffled along, passing between the vans. The warm air moved through the trees behind the motel, making them hiss. A flock of nightbirds passed above the robot with a whispering sigh.

He looked up, snapped a couple of infrared photos, and went back to his rounds. In a few minutes he slipped back into Sylvie's room. He stood in a corner and monitored her breath. Three more hours of sleep.

Outside, someone was walking beside one of the vans. Professor Digger did not hear.

Bones woke instantly when the hand clamped down over his mouth. It was pitch dark in the motel room, and he could hear someone snoring in the next bed. Marty.

Bones fought his instinct to struggle. If they wanted him dead, they could have done it already. If they wanted to talk, he decided it would be courteous to listen. After a long moment a raspy voice close to his ear said, "Dr. Bones, I presume. You don't know me, but we have a mutual friend. Carlos Janova?"

Bones nodded, as much as the powerful hand would allow.

"Listen to me, Dr. Bones," the raspy voice said. "Today there were more riots in the capital and other places. Do you know why? Because you said on the cube you knew the bones were faked."

Zeke lay still, remembering Sylvie's question a few hours earlier. How would he feel if war came to this planet because of something he discovered?

"I got the impression," said the raspy voice, "that you know who is behind these fakes. Do you?"

Bones didn't move. He might speculate like hell, but he didn't really *know.* He wasn't going to finger Kingsmill. Or Bart Charles, for that matter.

"All right," the man said. "I respect that. In the long run, it doesn't matter who did it. Your friend Carlos wanted us to lie down and wait to see what you would find out. I guess now we know. I guess now there is no reason to hold back."

Bones began to squirm. He made noises in his throat, but not loud ones. Marty snored on.

"Quietly," said the raspy voice. "And I *mean* it." He slowly lifted his hand from Zekes mouth.

Bones took a deep breath, then said, "It would be fatal to launch a full-scale attack against the government."

"That's what Janova said."

"He was right, and what's more, you won't *have* to fight. So what if a bunch of bones got faked? They can't last, they can't survive a full inquiry. Don't forget: your planet is full of bones, real bones, bones that will tell the truth. It's only a matter of time."

"In the time we wait, they are squeezing the life out of us, out of our planet. How can you ask us to wait?"

"Because if you attack now, you'll lose. And when the right bones come to the surface, it'll be too late. Sure, you'll have the law on your side, but they'll have your violent past to use against you. Sure, you'll get your planet back, but they'll make sure it takes forever."

The raspy voice laughed. "Carlos said that, too. What are you, brothers?"

"We're just reading from the same text. The book of reality."

The man was silent for so long that Bones was beginning to think he'd gone. Then: "We'll think about what you said. Close your eyes. Go to sleep. This is just a dream. Just a dream."

CHAPTER 20

Dawn was an hour away, and they all stumbled around the vans in the darkness, warming motors and checking equipment. Over mugs of scalding coffee Zeke had told them of his encounter with the raspy voice. Marty promptly declared it a dream, as no one could have gotten into that room without his knowledge. Sylvie, on the other hand, believed him; she just sulked because he hadn't alerted her somehow so she could get an interview. After that, it seemed to Bones that everybody was avoiding him.

Sylvie said, "I'm going to ride with Marty for a while. He says he wants a little company."

"Fine. Can you send one of your cameras with Professor Digger?"

"Yes, but you won't be able to get a live picture, if that's what you want. Not if he's on the highway, and we're running through the bushes, looking for a trail. We need line of sight."

"Oh, that's right, and there'll be some low hills between us."

"At least."

Sylvie suggested her camera could be set to make recordings which, if they were able to get some satellite time, could be downloaded later.

"I'll tell Kadak!xa to collect it for us," said Bones. "She hasn't had much to do this trip."

"Thank God."

"Uh . . ." It occurred to him she thought Kadak!xa was sitting up there in orbit ready to fire off lasers or something if they got into trouble. If Sylvie didn't know the *Ostrom* had been disarmed, this was not be a good time to tell her. "Right," he said. "Can you be ready in ten minutes?"

"Five. I'll call you from Marty's van."

"Good."

Zeke climbed into his cab. He got Digger on the radio and

confirmed the route with him. "Very well," said the robot.

In six minutes Sylvie checked in, and Digger's van pulled out, climbing back onto the highway. Doc revved his engine and drove off down a badly paved road that curved behind the motel and headed for the gray hills at the border of the Great Wilderness. Marty's van brought up the rear.

Zeke smiled, thinking of the little man and Sylvie riding together. He wondered if they were talking about him.

In two hours the day was bright and the sun was already hot. The trail was pretty good, running beneath the cover of the trees. It would take a damned fine recon satellite to pick them out in there.

(At random intervals, as her orbit permitted, Kadak!xa broadcast a cryptic, "No joy, no joy," meaning she had no visual contact. She knew approximately where to look, so if she couldn't see them, it was unlikely anybody could.)

Fuzzy black moss festooned the lower branches of the trees, drooping halfway to the ground. In places it nearly covered the dead-white bark of the trunks. Vines of a muddy yellow shade dangled from tree to tree. Grim, black-feathered birds roosted high in the treetops, not bothering to stir as the two vans passed beneath.

A moody, rather depressing place, thought Zeke.

From time to time they passed small piles of ancient, square-hewn stones. Parts of native shrines, perhaps, now tumbled into the undergrowth.

He wondered if Sylvie was getting any good footage. That is, if Marty hadn't put her to sleep with war stories and cooking tips.

Bart Charles sat in his temporary office in the capital, listening to his informant from the Earth consulate make a lot of dreary excuses.

"I can't imagine what went wrong," said Stallings Standford. "I leaked the story about the missing females, I even supplied the press with those x-rays you gave me. The resulting report was positively incendiary—yet the overall results were, well . . ."

"Disappointing?" said Charles.

"Yes."

There had been a few scattered riots, but no full-scale uprising. The rebels still waited to see what Bones would do. Disappointing? It was *infuriating*.

"Deliver a message to Kingsmill," said Charles. "I want him to find Dr. Bones and kill him. Make it look like rebel action. Maybe I can get the government pumped up enough to provoke these lazy rebels. Otherwise, I don't know what to do."

"Yes, sir," said Standford.

Bart Charles brooded. As long as Bones roamed free, he was a magnet for the real fossils. Keelor Ru must have heard about the Doc by now. Okay: they were watching Ru—he'd lead them to the bones.

"Get to work," he told Standford. "Tell Kingsmill they split up. One van's going up the highway, the other two—" Charles stopped. He'd already covered this.

"I'll tell him," said Standford.

Charles waved him off.

This project was jinxed, ever since Carlos Janova ran away to Earth. If he hadn't first confided in his friend Standford . . . well, it didn't matter. Bones had come to Garu'ka anyway. Charles would just have to deal with that. It was time to get this thing back on track.

By early afternoon the forest mist was rising again, and the surrounding trees were only vague shapes. Zeke had slowed down, and Marty's van was close behind. Maybe it would be a good time to stop. . . .

Kadak!xa's clattering voice filled the omni receiver. "Test results: three point five, plus or minus one point five, to the ninth, standard. Repeat . . ."

Bones never did hear the repeated words. His brain was noisy with the impossible. Three point five plus or minus one point five to the ninth. To the *ninth*! How could that be? How could the bones be between two and five *billion* years old?

Then he grinned.

Of course.

An hour later Marty got on the radio. "C'mon, boss. Let's break . . . before I embarrass myself."

Zeke grabbed the mike. "Whatever you say."

He pulled off the road into a wide area beneath a stand of tall trees. The mist had abated somewhat, and the late afternoon sun glowed through and filled the world with a warm golden light.

Zeke stayed in his cab a moment, making notes on the map. When at last he climbed down, he saw Marty coming through the mist from the direction of the trees. "Feel better now?"

Marty zipped his fly and grinned. "Almost human."

"An interesting statement. Where's Sylvie?"

Marty looked around. "I don't know. In the bushes, I guess. You want me to drag her out for you?"

Zeke shook his head. "Too dangerous."

"That's what I thought. Any word from Professor Digger?"

"No, but I wasn't expecting any."

"What was that thing on the radio a while back? Cryptic numbers."

"Test results," said Bones. "I had Kadak!xa try something for me."

"Three point five billion. Is that years?"

"Yep. They screwed up. Somehow, improbable as it sounds, they seem to have anticipated my test. They must have exposed the bones to neutrino radiation—but they cooked 'em too long."

"I'll say."

Doc looked out into the misty bushes. "She's sure taking her time."

Marty followed his gaze. There was nothing moving out there. "Well, that's the way it works sometimes."

"You're getting philosophical." Zeke reached into his van and grabbed a sandwich. Tossing it to Marty, he said, "Here. I expect Sylvie's eaten all your reserves."

The little man tore eagerly at the wrapping. "Don't be silly. Nobody touches my reserves."

While he chewed—and made happy groaning noises—Zeke kept watching the bushes. He checked his watch.

"Been five minutes."

"She's all right. Take care of yourself. Or don't you excrete anymore?"

"I'm just afraid if I go out there now I'll run into her."

Marty laughed, his voice sounding loud in the enveloping mist. "You should have watched which way she went."

Zeke stared at him. "What do you mean? She's not riding with me."

"Yes, she is."

"No, no. She said she—she said you wanted—" Zeke looked off into the mist. "Sylvie!" he yelled. "Answer me right now!"

There was no response.

"You think I'm kidding?" said Marty.

Zeke pulled open the van door and looked in the camper section. He popped back out and said, "Look in the back of your van."

"There's nobody in there, boss."

"Go look!"

"I know what happened," said Marty, backing up slowly. "She went with Digger. She went to get some footage of the ambush."

"She wouldn't . . ."

"The hell she wouldn't."

"Will you please just go look?"

But before Marty could get very far Zeke's radio squawked into life. "Professor Digger calling Dr. Bones." The robot's voice was ripped with static. "We're on the dirt road, coordinates in code." The radio squealed for a second. "Blockade ahead. Native gentlemen are approaching. They're painted green and yellow. They have weapons. They—"

His voice cut off and Sylvie yelled, "Get over here fast, Zeke! They look like they're gonna—"

The transmission died abruptly.

"I knew it!" yelled Marty, as he ran to his van.

Zeke started to climb into the cab, hesitated, stepped up, and stopped, groaning. He dropped back to the dirt, unzipping his pants. "Damned plumbing . . ."

CHAPTER 21

Chill drops of water were falling from someplace high above, hitting the stone floor beside her head with precise regularity. Tiny flecks of water exploded from each splash, touching her face like a cool mist. She stirred, and rolled her aching head. Now the drops were landing on her forehead with the force of small wet stones. She groaned and rolled away. Water trickled down the slopes of her face. She sighed . . . and slowly woke to the worst headache of her life.

"Oh, God . . ." she muttered, prying herself off the cold floor. It was dark in there, but faint yellow light crept into the room through the bars of the door. She could hear voices outside: male voices, grumbling, laughing, arguing voices. She remembered the painted Garukan's who had swarmed over the van so suddenly.

They had her. Now what?

She got on her knees and crawled closer to the dripping water, which made loud plopping noises as it slammed into the damp stones. She reached out, filled her palms with water, and wet her face, her throat, the back of her neck. Her head continued to bang as if her brain wanted out.

They hit me, she thought.

She remembered now, how they reached in and grabbed her away from the radio mike. One of them raised his arm and clouted her with the heavy butt of a large knife. Someone was yelling for him to stop, but he didn't. She found herself recording the incident as if it were happening to somebody else. She counted two blows before she faded. There might have been more.

Sylvie held another handful of cold water to her face and rubbed it in, trying to bring herself back from the dead. She looked up, but couldn't see where the water came from. The ceiling was too far away, and the room was too dark.

What *was* this place?

She tried to remember the map. They had been stopped about two-thirds of the way up the dirt road to the digging site. There was something nearby, on the left of the road, down a trail. A stone temple.

That was it. A large stone temple, now tumbled to ruins. Somebody had told her how stupid it was for them to build the road so close to the temple. Even though the site had been abandoned hundreds of years ago, it was still a sacred place to the natives, and the Cultural Committee or whoever it was that had planned the access road should have given it wider berth. She remembered somebody telling her that, Zeke?

Probably Zeke. He was always so full of answers. The guy seemed to know everything.

He was the guy who said she couldn't stay with Digger and cover the ambush. No, wait, he hadn't said that. She had never asked him. Yeah, that's right. She had decided there was no point in asking him. She knew what the answer would be. And there was no sense tipping him off that she was even *thinking* such a thing.

But she not only thought about it, she did it. And look how well everything had turned out. . . .

Damn it, he was gonna yell at her this time. Oh God, was he gonna yell!

She sat up, groaning softly.

If she got out of this alive. . . .

Keelor Ru kept waking and falling asleep. He was on the floor by the wall, curled up on the filthy rug. He'd been there all night and all day, drifting in and out of sleep until his head felt stuffed with cotton. He stank of sweat that had dried and gone damp again. The room was still hot, the air close. He opened his eyes and looked across the darkness without moving his head. Faint light played across the still curtains, neon reds and greens. He guessed it was full dark outside.

His eyelids drooped shut again.

A hundred dream images leaped and cavorted in front of him, tormenting and real. It was as though his mind were waiting in the dark to destroy him with angry dreams.

He opened his eyes again, fought to keep them open.

He thought: I have wasted my life. And now they are going to kill me. They are going to kill me before I can do a thing to redeem my wasted life.

Redemption.

There it was again, that word. As if there was anything he could do . . .

He stared at the lights caught in the weave of the curtains. He almost smiled. There *was* something he could do. Something easy and well within his failed powers. Something for which they could only kill him . . . and they were going to do that anyway.

All he had to do was find a phone and call Dr. Bones. Tell him where the fossils are, sit down, and wait for the skull piercing bullet. Dead easy.

The question was: Could he do it? Could he do this one simple thing?

He concluded he could not.

Because the first step in carrying out this wonderful and redeeming action, this first, utterly cinch step, was to get up off the floor. And he knew he could never do that. He knew he would never move again. Not a centimeter. There was no point in trying a thing. He was paralyzed.

Keelor Ru sighed. Dust blew up from his breath—and he sneezed. He coughed, then he sneezed again, banging his head on the hardwood floor. "Damn it!" he said, automatically rolling to a sitting position. He sneezed again, bit his tongue, and swore, rather loudly. It was almost funny.

Outside his room the floorboards creaked, and he didn't even turn to listen. The hell with them. He was already dead. What did he care?

Keelor Ru stood up and walked to the window. He pulled the curtain back and looked. Yes, there he was, standing in the mouth of the alley: the man who had come to kill him. Screw him. Ru waved, and the man backed into the alley, into the shadows.

Keelor Ru started to laugh—and stopped. Wait a minute. If they knew where he was, why hadn't they killed him already?

"Oh, yeah," he muttered.

The bones. They must be hoping he'd lead them to the bones. Well, that wasn't going to happen.

Somewhere in that explosive, unavoidable series of sneezes, Keelor Ru had made up his mind. If he was already dead—and this he could not doubt, not with *his* enemies—then he might as well get some things done. Because he was already dead, he had become, in a twisted sense, invincible.

Keelor Ru went into the bathroom, stripped down, showered, and shaved. He trotted back into the room, naked, wet hair slicked back, and dug around in his bag for clean underwear. Might as well do this right.

As he was buttoning up his fresh shirt, he chanced to look out the window. Now there were *two* of them, carved in relief by the shadow's knife. They seemed to be arguing. One of them pointed up at the window. Keelor waved again. The men were too busy to notice. Keelor Ru laughed and went back into the bathroom to brush his teeth and comb his hair.

He grabbed his money (he still had quite a wad left over from cleaning out his bank account), but left the rest of his stuff—he wouldn't need it anymore. He checked the window one last time. Both men were gone.

Keelor Ru smiled. Time to go, brother.

The hallway was deserted, but there were noises on the stairs below, coming this way. Keelor Ru strode to the stairs and looked down. Yep.

He crossed the landing and began climbing, trying not to make too much noise, but not making a big deal about being quiet, either. Somehow he knew that if he ever once let himself worry or second guess his instincts, he'd be screwed. He'd be petrified with fear—and there was no future in that. He had work to do.

Above the top floor the stairs continued, dead-ending at a single steel door. He unlatched it and went out onto the flat roof of the hotel. It was dark as hell, but he kept on going, making his way to the crumbling edge. The roof of the next building was several meters away and lower than this one. A guy could get killed jumping that gap, killed *easy*.

Without hesitation he stepped back and took a run at it. That short moment in midair, suspended with the dark, cooling breeze in his face, was like all the good times of the last five years compressed into a giddy lump and handed to him. He had to laugh.

Flat out on his stomach, Marty took another squint through the nightscope. "Nobody's around."

Zeke was right beside him, monitoring the tracker. "Doesn't matter. They're in there."

From here atop the grassy slope the stone temple dimly glistened in the light of the misty stars. Most of a tower was still standing, along with a larger building, the entrance of which was a wide arch atop a long staircase. In the distance another such staircase led nowhere, a large field of blocky stones spread out beyond. Three other buildings were seen, smaller, roofless, walls crumbling in ancient lines, straight and curved.

"I can see carvings around the entrance," said Marty. "Large birds, guys with the heads of lizards, the sun rising over a hill, more guys fighting with triangular swords. We should get some pix of this."

"Later," said Doc. "Gimme the 'scope." He searched the ruins himself. It was dead quiet.

Marty said, "We go down there, right?"

"I guess so. Have you got anything we could use as a weapon?"

"I got that big screwdriver."

"What else?"

"A jumbo tube of Rodale's Superglue."

"Oh, *that'll* come in handy."

"Well, you never know what—"

"*Shhhh!*"

Someone was coming up behind them, walking noisily over the uneven ground.

Keelor Ru fed coins into the phone until the directory's screen lit up. It had been in the news that Dr. Ezekiel Bones was staying in the capital at the high security estate of industrialist Warren Kingsmill. Ru typed the name into the keyboard and waited. A moment later the screen flashed the bad news. Kingsmill's number wasn't listed.

"Damn," he muttered.

He tried to think if there was anybody else he could call. All his friends had scattered, and he couldn't call the local cops, that was certain. Maybe they were corrupt and maybe they weren't. He couldn't take any chances.

After a long moment he hung up. The directory went dark, and a rattle of coins filled the metal trough.

Okay, he'd have to find Bones in person. There was no question the man would listen to him. Bones had even gone on the cube, saying the fossils were probably fakes. Right, so what would he say if the real ones were dropped in his lap?

Keelor Ru walked on down the dark street, planning it out. First, he needed to pick up that black market car. Then he'd have to go by the hiding place and collect a sample of the bones, in case the big time doctor needed a little persuasion. Find the man, astonish him with the fossils, and relax in the glow of victory. It was going to be easy.

He walked until he came to an area where fences lined the street: wire barriers that kept the trash from getting mixed in with the good junk—the wrecked machines of an ending era, semi-useless trinkets from the United Worlds, bright baubles designed to astound the fawning natives.

He knew all that was coming to an end now . . . one way or another.

Without warning a large gray dog charged at him from across the street. It came snarling: a low, grim rumbling sound in its chest.

Keelor turned, said, "Stop now!" in the local dialect.

The dog skidded to a halt and blinked at him. Keelor smiled and walked on. You just have to know how to talk to them.

Sylvie sat on the cold stone floor for a long time, holding her head in her hands, feeling it throb, trying to keep awake. She began to wonder why she was still alive. She remembered the voice, yelling for the guy to stop hitting her. It must have worked—but how long would this spell of protection last?

Outside her cell they were still arguing, their voices incomprehensible. Was it a debate? If so, how soon before they decided—and what would they do?

What would *they* do?

The thought was like an electric goad. What the hell did she care what *they* decided?

"Come on, Sylvie," she muttered. "You're in control here."

Think.

Think.

Think of a way out.

Her mind was a blank.

She wanted to start planning something, to get something going, to take some action, to do *any* thing but sit there and wait for somebody else to decide her life—but she couldn't concentrate. Her head pounded away like mad, and her eyes kept closing.

I'm in shock, she thought. That bastard brained me, and now my body wants to roll over and go to sleep. My body wants to give up. My body wants to drop dead.

"Yeah, well *I* don't!"

She went shakily to the cell door and looked out into a stone corridor, lit by electric torches from another room. The voices were louder, but still they made no sense. Please, God, she prayed. Let it be a foreign language, and not my brain crapping out.

She tested the door, found it impossibly sturdy. All right, okay, you just have to expect that from a cell door. Keep going.

She turned, groaning as the motion squeezed her fragile head. She resolved to search her dark cell for something that could help her escape.

But the first thing she did was fall flat on her face. Her head blew up like a balloon and popped. She swore and crawled back to destroy whatever it was that had tripped her.

Hello, Professor Digger.

CHAPTER 22

Zeke and Marty lay on the grassy slope, listening to the noise of someone coming up toward them in the dark. A shape crossed in front of the stars, suddenly very near. It stopped. Zeke held his breath. It was so dark on the hillside that he was convinced whoever it was could not see them, though they were only a few meters away. Nothing happened. They could hear the person breathing, weight shifting on the sandy gravel of the trail.

This is ridiculous, thought Zeke.

He slowly rolled over, raised the nightscope to his eyes—and yelled.

Marty screamed in response.

The intruder screamed and started to run back down the slope. Zeke jumped up and collided with Marty. Five meters away the intruder tripped, hit the ground hard, and started to cry.

"Damn it!" yelled Doc, as quietly as he could. "Don't cry! It's all right!"

He yanked the flashlight off his belt and flicked on the red blackout beam. Marty grabbed the back of his shirt and they went down the slope to where Merrily Kingsmill lay sprawled on the ground, sobbing.

"It's us!" said Zeke, shining the light on himself and Marty.

Merrily looked up, the red light reflecting in her eyes. "I got scared," she said, "waiting in the van."

"You mean 'hiding' in the van," Zeke said. "Marty's van."

"Hey, don't look at me," said Marty. "I didn't know she was in there."

"You were probably chewing too loud to hear her."

"I thought it would be fun," said Merrily, getting to her feet.

"What are we going to do with her?" asked Marty.

"I don't know. We've got work to do."

"Lock her in the van."

"No!" she said.

"Quiet!" said Zeke, flicking off the light.

"Don't yell at me!"

Marty said, "I could cold-cock her, boss. That'd quiet her down."

"Just you *try* it!" she said, in a vicious tone of voice that made Marty back up in a hurry.

"Sorry, Red. Just kidding."

"Okay, then."

"We *could* leave her on the hill with the nightscope," said Zeke. "You wanna be our lookout?"

"Lookout for what?"

"I'll show you."

Doc led her back to the top of the hill. She stretched out beside him while he scanned the temple grounds again. Nothing had changed. He handed her the 'scope and showed her how to focus.

"There's nobody down there," she said, after a short search.

"They're in there, someplace," said Zeke. "Sylvie and our robot—they were ambushed by . . . rebels . . . or natives . . . or somebody."

He wished he could call Kadak!xa to get a heatscan of the area, but the *Ostrom* was on the farside right now and he didn't want to wait.

Marty handed her a small transceiver. "If you see anybody moving around down there, call us."

Zeke flicked on the blackout light. "Show her how to operate the radio."

"Okay, look," said Marty. "We've got a matched-frequency pair here, so don't worry about the channel. Here's the transmit button. Push to talk, release to listen. This is the volume control."

"Got it," said Merrily.

Zeke killed the light. He pulled out the tracker and confirmed the signal. "Let's go."

"Good luck!" she said.

They were halfway down the hill when Marty grabbed Zeke and whispered, "I *hate* it when they say 'good luck.'"

Zeke didn't answer. In another minute they were entering the field of stones, where large, angular blocks poked up through the muddy soil.

· · ·

"That's close enough," said a gruff voice.

Keelor Ru stopped. A thickset figure in a long overcoat stood in the half-opened gateway. Through the wire fence Keelor could see vague heaps of mounded junk, bits of metal gleaming coldly in the dim light.

"I mean it," said the big guy. He reached dramatically into the dark folds of his overcoat, as if going for a gun.

"Cut the crap, Novas," said Keelor Ru. "I don't believe you've carried a gun in your whole life. I'm in kind of a hurry, so could we just—"

The big guy moved closer. "Keelor Ru?"

"What's left of him."

"I expected you three days ago."

"I took a break. Is the car ready?"

"I don't know."

"You know."

Keelor stepped past him and kept right on going, into the junkyard. Novas could only follow. "In the back," he said, finally. They walked past broken-down androids, rusting vendo-bots, and gutted servomechs.

"Tell your fortune?" asked an android crone dressed as a gypsy. The lower half of her body was a tangled landslide of gears and motors. "Tell your fortune," she repeated, one eye winking erratically.

"It's this damned mist," said Novas. "The moisture sets her going."

"I see *death*," the android said. "The bones of loved ones strewn about."

Keelor Ru laughed. "I like it."

They moved on, passing heaps of cannibalized gambling machines. Keelor stooped to snatch an old coin from the dust, saying, "My lucky day." He kept on walking, then had to wait for Novas to catch up. "Find any yourself?"

Novas shook his head, looking pissed. "Turn left up here."

Cars lined the path on both sides, stacked five high, full of empty headlight sockets and grinning grillwork.

"Now right," said Novas.

There was a kind of tunnel through the junk. Keelor asked, "How's this car run?"

"Like a champ."

"I'm counting on you."

"Of course, I understand."

At the end of the line was a single row of unlicensed cars, sitting on their tires.

"Don't tell me it's one of these."

"Hey, I know they don't look like much, but—"

"You're kidding—it *is* one of these?"

"Cosmetically they're not so hot, but—"

"All right, which one? Can I pick my own?"

"Sure, if you don't mind working all night on it. This one needs a tranny, this one a fuel cell, this one a new electrical system . . ."

"I get it. Is there one of these ready to go?"

"I said I had one, didn't I?"

Novas walked to the fourth car in the line, a dark gray, badly dented, bloated heap of a car.

"You're kidding."

"Plenty of cargo space," said Novas.

Keelor lifted his empty arms. "I'm traveling light, you know?"

"You might pick somebody up," said Novas, winking.

Keelor Ru laughed. "All right, fine, I don't want to argue. Does it run?"

Novas looked hurt.

"Sorry," said Ru. "Two weeks ago you said ten, I gave you half, I owe you five thousand. Right?" He started to peel off the bills.

"Uh . . ."

Keelor stopped. "I don't like the sound of that."

"I'm going to need twenty," said Novas. "That's fifteen more you owe me."

"More late night jokes."

"I mean it. This here's a prime piece of transportation."

"And I'm a prime piece of easy mark, right? You figure, guy's on the run, guy needs a car, guy's gonna pay anything I ask."

"I got expenses, Ru. I take chances too, you know."

Keelor smiled. "You son of a bitch."

Novas shrugged.

Keelor said, "Did it ever occur to you that a desperado might just take the car without paying you a thing?"

"You wouldn't do that."

"What makes you so sure?"

Novas jerked his head, and Keelor looked. There was a large

black dog moving stiffly toward him from the shadows, growling faintly, long white teeth exposed.

"I'm not worried," said Keelor. "I got a way with dogs."

"Don't be confused," said Novas. "That's not a real dog."

Keelor looked again—and *listened*. The dog was not growling; what he heard was the sound of churning motors.

"He's a killer," said Novas. "Programmed him myself."

"Oh hell, he'd fall apart if I *sneezed* on him."

"Oh, yeah?" Novas sounded hurt again.

"Tell you what I'm going to do," said Keelor, peeling off six bills. "Here's the five I owe you . . . and another thousand for the dog. Buy him something nice."

Novas didn't move, so Keelor stuffed the money in the breast pocket of the guy's overcoat. He went over to the car.

"You'll never find the keys!" said Novas.

"They're in the ignition," said Keelor, climbing through the window. The cars were parked so close together he couldn't open the door.

Novas came forward. "I got expenses."

"You got balls," said Keelor. "Keep 'em away from your dog."

He cranked up the car and listened to the motor. A little sour, but what the hell. He rolled the beast forward, Novas backing up.

The dog tried to back up, too, but got his legs tangled and fell over, paws twitching. Novas hurried over to set him upright and point him out of harm's way.

Keelor guided the car back through the junkyard. The gate was still half open; a little nudge with the front of the car and he had enough room to get out. Novas came trotting up behind him. "I gave you a good deal!" he yelled. "Remember that!"

"Go back to sleep," said Keelor Ru, turning into the road.

The streets were deserted as he made his way out of town, headed for the Great Wilderness.

Zeke held the tracker up where he could see it. "Very close now," he whispered.

They were inside the temple's big building, easing down a long flight of slippery stone stairs, moving deeper and deeper into the sub-basement. The place was divided into multiple cells— small rooms with ceilings that reached right through the gutted basement and into the second floor of the building.

Marty banged into Zeke's back again. The little man no longer bothered to apologize. Doc reached back and grabbed his arm. "They're in the next room," he said, so quietly he wasn't sure he could hear the words himself.

Marty nodded vaguely in the darkness. The sub-basement was dead silent.

Zeke paused outside the last cell, wondering if he would feel any better with Marty's big screwdriver in his hand. The dwarf collided with him again, and Zeke bounded forward, into the cell. It was empty.

Zeke looked around. The tracker's signal was beeping frantically in his earpiece. He shut it off. "I don't get it," he whispered, louder this time.

"I do," said Marty, stooping to pick something up.

Zeke opened the flashlight's red beam. "Damn . . ."

It was the robot's ping'r. Someone had ripped it loose and tossed it down there. Bones took it, looked it over, and shut it down. "Natives?"

"They couldn't have known."

"That's what I mean," said Zeke. "Somebody's helping them. I got a feeling we might run up against the guys behind this tonight."

"Kingsmill?"

"Yeah, he's on the short list." Zeke looked at the silent tracker in his hand. "Okay, now what?"

The tracker bleeped nicely, the target light flickering in the grid. Novas grinned and bent to pat his whirring guard dog on the head—*clunk, clunk.*

He crossed his rusting steel cabin and sat down in a creaky lounge chair. In front of him was the picturephone, an ancient thing in a cracked plastic case. The screen didn't light up anymore, and whoever had thrown it out had gutted the camera for parts. But it still hooked up to the phone-net okay, and sometimes it even beeped with a call for him.

Novas tapped out the number they'd given him. After a minute a voice answered. "Go ahead."

"This is Novas. He just left."

"Have you got a signal?"

"Yes, sir."

"Wait a minute."

Novas waited while the guy got his own tracker activated.

"We have him."

"Is everything all right?"

The voice laughed. "You want the bonus, right?"

"I earned it."

"You'll get it."

The phone went dead.

Novas put the tracker away and went looking for a nice cup of three-bean soup. Not a bad night, after all.

CHAPTER 23

Keelor Ru fought the wheel of the car. The new road was already rutted by the run-off from spring rains, and every time the front wheels of the car hit one of the ruts, the steering wheel lurched and spun, and the car shimmied dangerously close to the trees that lined the road.

He smiled, shaking his head. The car Novas had sold him was a piece of junk after all. The motor had already cut out twice, and though the aircirc system clattered and wheezed, it delivered no air.

The hell with it. He hadn't expected to get this far anyway. It was a miracle they hadn't trapped him in his room and blown his sorry head off. He was living a sort of supernatural mission— that he had been killed, but then had been sent back to life to redeem his miserable soul.

Keelor Ru gunned the engine, forcing the big car around a rockslide. Dirt flew into the darkness, spun by tires that whined and slipped and then regained their grip. The car jerked forward, sliding, and hit the road again.

He glanced in the rearview mirror. The road behind him was pitch black, but a horrible thought occurred to him. What if they let him go on purpose? He slowed the car, not knowing what to do. Could they be following?

The car rolled slower and slower in the dirt, the singing note of the engine winding down. He stopped. Outside the car the night creatures rattled through the trees.

Keelor Ru slumped forward, gripping the wheel tightly. The old fear was rising from the darkness, reaching out, reaching for *him* . . .

He yelled and stomped the accelerator. The car lurched forward, sliding in the loose gravel. Tires bit, and the car took off.

He knew what he had to do now. He had to outrace the fear that loped up the road toward him. He'd gotten out of that hotel room on pure, deadman bravado—and that was the juice that was going to get him where he needed to go. If they were after him, fine—that was their business. Dead guys lacked finesse: they blustered their way through. They didn't stop to worry.

"You can't touch me," he said. "I'm already a ghost."

Dr. Darma paced the length of Kingsmill's living room. "I don't see why we have to wait. We've got a good tracking signal on him right now. He must be headed for the bones."

"Sit down," said Kingsmill. He waved his jiggling glass. "Have a drink. You know where everything is."

"A drink?"

"Yeah, you need relaxing. Besides, all this pacing, back and forth, back and forth . . . you're making me dizzy."

Darma pointed at the glass in the man's hand. "You're always dizzy."

Kingsmill watched him. "You talk like a rich man, Darma. Which you are not. *Richer*, maybe—since you met me—but you seem to think a little money has made you smarter. It hasn't, believe me."

The Garukan stopped pacing. "I am the chairman of the Cultural Commission. Nobody questions my ability to—"

"Oh, shut up, Darma. You're a cheap hustler and you know it. If you *don't* know it, you're even dumber than I thought." Kingsmill stared at him. "You might even be too dumb to trust."

Darma started to say something, then stopped. He walked to the end of the room, turned, and came back.

Kingsmill pointed at him. "What did I say?"

Darma hesitated, and found a chair to sit in. "He's getting away."

"No, he's not," said Kingsmill, sipping his drink. "And to answer your earlier question, we're waiting for my partner."

Darma stood up. Kingsmill glanced at him, and he sat back down. "Sorry."

From outside came a buzzing sound, and the trees of the compound began to sway. Kingsmill gestured with his glass. "See, that wasn't so long to wait, was it?"

Bart Charles brought some of his armed men with him. And Colonel Escont. "Where's Bones?" asked Charles.

"We still don't know," said Kingsmill. "But the trap's set.

Baviera hid the robot's ping'r in a ruined temple. One of his best men is watching the place."

"Good."

"And we've got a strong track signal on Keelor Ru."

Charles nodded. "All right, let's get organized."

Zeke keyed his radio and asked Merrily to come down. "What did you find?" she asked, picking her way through the stones.

"Nobody's here," said Bones.

"What are we going to do now?"

"I don't know."

"We'll look for tire tracks," said Marty, grabbing the flashlight. He put the beam on high white and started off, moving close to the ground, which was easy for him.

Merrily took Zeke's arm. "I guess you're pretty mad I'm here."

"I'm . . . confused . . . is all. Why didn't you ask if you could come along? We probably would have . . . well, we *might* have let you come."

"Yeah, but my dad wouldn't. And I don't think you would have said okay if he was against it."

Zeke nodded, wondering how much to tell Merrily about her father. He still had no real proof, but as time went on, it was possible they'd run into the guy doing something unforgivable. Should he warn her?

"Your dad had a hunting lodge out here somewhere, right?"

"It's east of the Wilderness. About fifty kilometers from here . . . I think. This is the big temple, isn't it? And that road is the one that leads to the digging site?"

"You remember the maps. I didn't think you were paying attention."

"I'm not as stupid as you think."

"I never said you were."

"Hey!" said Marty, his voice muted. "Come over here. *Quietly.*"

Zeke and Merrily tiptoed over, stumbling on the uneven blocks. Marty pointed behind a large rock. There was a native Garukan lying there, his face painted to look ferocious. He was asleep, snoring softly. Beside him was an empty bottle of hooch and a two-way radio.

"A guard," said Marty.

"Waiting for us," said Bones.

At that moment they all heard a droning engine sound, and Marty doused the light. The sound got louder, coming their way. "This place is getting busy," said Zeke.

Lights glowed in the distance, throbbing and shifting behind the trees. The native continued to snore.

"Whoever he is," said Marty, "he's driving like a maniac."

In moments the headlights broke free of the background shining clear, obscuring the car with the glare.

"Behind these rocks!" yelled Zeke, and everybody dived into the tall grass. The car's engine boomed, its tires sang and hissed on the gravel, coming closer.

At the last minute the native guard woke and jumped up into the light, looking panicked. He ran a few meters away from the light, searching for a place to hide. He discovered Bones and company, yelling in surprise. "Find your own place," said Marty, waving his big screwdriver. The native ran away backwards, totally freaked.

The car leapt around a boulder, motor screaming, tires throwing dirt in the air. The Garukan spun around, yelled once, and ran off into the trees as the car zoomed past.

It was a big gray hog of a car—a real piece of junk. The three of them stood and watched the taillights fade into the distance. The woods grew quiet again.

"He was really in a big hurry," said Merrily.

"If it's *that* important," said Zeke, "we ought to check it out."

Marty went over and stomped the native's radio into the grass. "In case he comes back."

They took off up the grassy hill, running for the vans.

CHAPTER 24

Manel Baviera pushed the button on the radio, holding it a little way from his face as he did so. He yelled at the thing, "Tell me all that again!"

After a moment he remembered to let go of the button. The radio coughed and hissed, then Kingsmill's voice said, "There is someone coming your way in a beat-up car. Tell your men to go down the road and watch for him. Don't interfere with him. We want to know exactly where he goes."

Baviera pushed the button and yelled, "Okay!"

He released it again and waited. "That's not all," said the crackling voice. "We have now decided. Kill the girl and destroy the robot. Do this right away. Do you understand?"

Baviera thought about asking for more money, but it was too much trouble talking through this stupid machine. Okay, he'd kill the girl and eat the difference.

Kingsmill was still squawking at him. "—hear from your ambush site?"

Baviera pushed the button. "What? Oh, nothing. He hasn't reported a thing. Okay, boss. I'll talk to you when you get here."

The radio hissed again and was silent. Baviera threw it into a leather pouch he wore on a strap around his neck. He was dressed—or rather undressed—and painted to look like an authentic Wilderness native. The real natives laughed at him; most of them had turned up wearing jeans and tennis shoes. No problem—Baviera showed them how to dress, that's what he was going to get. If the boss wanted natives with painted bodies, that's what he was going to get.

Baviera grabbed five guys and sent them down the road to wait for the maniac in the junker car. Then he rounded up two more to go with him to kill the girl and break the robot into bite-sized chunks.

"Come on, come on, come on!" he yelled, waving his arms. The natives smirked and moved slower yet.

Baviera took a big breath and blew it out in a sigh. It had been a long day full of headaches, but he wasn't complaining. Politics was a pretty good living.

Sylvie pounded Digger's copper skull. "What the hell's the matter with you? Why didn't you *tell* me you were in here? Hey, *answer* me!"

The professor ignored her questions. A short inspection told her why. Digger's chest had been opened, his main power switch shut down.

She toggled the switch, then jumped out of the way while he flailed about, banging his arms and legs on the stone floor.

"Stop it!" she hissed, her head pounding.

He mumbled and squeaked, quieting down. His limbs slowed to a quiver.

"Do you know who I am?" she asked.

"I am Professor Digger."

"Not you, *me*. Do you recognize me?"

"Oh no, it's the *mean* one!"

"I am *not* the mean one."

After a moment he said, "I stand corrected. You are Miss Sylvie Pharr." His voice matched hers: "'The best damned reporter on this end of the galaxy.'"

"I sound pretty snotty."

"I would not venture to make a judgment, Miss Pharr."

"Are you all right?"

"Just a minute. I'll look." The robot's eyes flickered for several seconds, then he said, "I've lost much of my power charge, and my emergency ping'r is missing, but other than that . . . I feel pretty chipper."

"Do you remember what happened to us?"

"Marauders, miss. They blocked the van with a fallen tree. And when I went out to move it—*blam!*"

"We managed to get some warning on the air, but I don't know if it did any good." She looked at the barred door. "They're out there somewhere, hear 'em? I got a feeling they plan to kill us . . . kill *me*, I mean."

"Just a theory, you understand," said Digger. "And I acknowledge that your intuitive processes may well be superior to mine —but it occurs to me that when they come to kill us—kill *you*, I mean—it might be an excellent situation if we were not here."

"You're absolutely right. Any ideas?"

Digger sat up straight. "May I be so bold?"

"I insist."

The van's headlights cut through the mist. Bushes and tree branches swept by like ghosts: barely seen and gone in an instant.

"Faster!" said Marty.

Zeke growled. "If you say that *one* more time . . . !"

Merrily sat in the middle. Zeke could feel her flinching with every lurch of the van.

After a while the road ran straight. It got very wide, trees dropping away into the darkness.

"What's this?" said Marty.

The corner of a wire fence flashed before them and the road curved violently. Marty yelled as the van slewed around on the loose gravel. Zeke pulsed the brakes, steadied the wheel, and brought the van to a stop, bouncing gently off the chain-link fence.

Dead end.

He killed the lights and they all jumped out. Fine white dust flowed like smoke through the flimsy barrier. In the dim distance they could see several steel-sided buildings.

"Elliot's dig site," said Zeke. "Standford said it was closed." He moved close to the gate and aimed his light at the lock. "Nothing busted. I don't think he went in here."

"Maybe he had a key," said Marty.

"Why is it so dark in there?" asked Merrily.

Zeke turned off his light and they stood for a long moment in the spooky darkness. He could hear the hum of a suppressor field, which meant guards were not needed. "I don't think anybody's in there."

"What's that smell?" asked Marty, sniffing the dirt.

Zeke reached for a handful and smelled it. "Ha. Our old friend, 2,4,5-trichloropheoxyacetic acid."

"What?" asked Merrily.

"It's a herbicide," said Bones. "Why is a known human teratogen used on this planet, when it's banned just about everyplace else?"

"Why?" asked Marty.

"Because it doesn't bother the Garukans a bit."

"Why not?" asked Merrily.

"Because they're not humans."

Marty laughed, something like a small dog's bark.

"It's not proof," said Bones, dusting off his hands. "But it's interesting."

The two vehicles tore through the night. Up front was the guncar, lightly armored, full of hard-assed men under the command of Colonel Escont. Behind them, wallowing in the loose gravel, was Kingsmill's limo.

It was close in the limo. Kingsmill and Bart Charles and Dr. Darma in the back, a driver and two of Charles's hired gunmen in front. The beeping sound of the tracker blended with the whine of the tires and the clicking of branches that whipped the sides of the car.

The men up front were silent, intent on their jobs. In the backseat Charles talked quietly and insistently at Kingsmill. Darma felt carsick from the swerving motion of the car. He sat turned toward the window with his eyes clamped shut.

Welcome to the big time.

He wished he were back in his little shop, hawking bogus bone trinkets. Nobody ever got killed. . . .

Baviera stationed his fellows outside the cell door. He checked through the grate, but it was so damned dark in there he couldn't make out a thing. Oh, well, swing the door and use the spotlight. He unhooked the powerful lamp from his belt and motioned to the guy with the key to undo the padlock. The door creaked open, and he hit the switch, whipping the light back and forth right near the door, wary of counter-ambushes. There was nobody there . . . not at either side . . . and not above the door, waiting to drop down on him.

He moved grimly forward, the natives at his back (and didn't *that* feel comfy). He swung the lamp around, quickly at first, then—as his anger grew—slowly and with great precision, careful not to miss a single dark corner.

Because the damned cell was empty.

"Oh, this is just perfect."

CHAPTER 25

Manel Baviera went around the inside of the cell, examining every square centimeter. He cursed as he went, and the natives stayed out of his way. Not only were the girl and the robot gone, there was no sign of how they managed it.

Manel went back to the door and examined the lock again. There had been no tampering. Baviera raged and looked for someone to hit.

He sent two of the natives into the catacombs to search, then he sat down for a moment to think. Could he possibly keep this little disaster quiet? Kingsmill was a powerful man in some ways. If he couldn't punish Baviera himself, he could certainly *hire* somebody to do it.

Manel groaned and hauled the radio out. He pushed the damned button. "Hello, Kingsmill. This is Baviera. I have to tell you. She's gone, and the robot, too."

He thought the boss would yell at him but he didn't. Manel waited, his thick fingers wrapped around the radio, holding the button in. After a long time he said, "Did you hear me, boss? The woman has escaped."

Still no answer. Baviera banged the radio against the stone wall, then listened some more. He shrugged, turned the radio off, and put it away. He had to think this whole thing out some more. Could it be the boss didn't care?

"Try again," said Bart Charles.

"I know what it is," said Kingsmill. "That primitive idiot is holding the transmit button down. I could hear him breathing."

"Try again," said Charles. "I don't want any loose ends."

Dr. Darma shifted around in the limo, moving closer to the cool window glass—as if he could distance himself from what was happening now.

Kingsmill held the radio up. "Baviera! Baviera!"

Darma waited, listening despite himself.

"I think he's turned the damned thing off," said Kingsmill.

"You hire good people," said Charles.

"I didn't hear you complain about the job he did on those two . . . bone donors."

Charles said nothing.

Darma was remembering that horrible day. He'd gone eagerly into Kingsmill's deserted shop: some old leased building full of filthy machinery. He'd assumed they'd collected a bunch of random bones from someplace, maybe out of Harden Merck's shop, if that geezer was still around. But when he saw what they had, laid out on those steel tables under the bright lights, he was sick. And when Charles handed him that power scalpel—

Darma's head jerked in recoil, banging his face on the hard glass. He could still hear them laughing, Charles and Kingsmill, as they pointed at Darma's blanched face. Monsters, they were monsters. And they *owned* him.

The limo swerved and vibrated, sending physical shocks through his skull and down his neck, down into the hidden bones of his body.

Into the bones . . .

"I got him!" said Kingsmill.

"About time," said Bart Charles.

Kingsmill yelled into the radio. "You listen to me, Baviera—and keep your finger off the button until I tell you. I want that woman found and killed. And if you find out who released her, kill *him*, too. I'm getting sick of your ineptitude. You're being paid a lot of money for a few simple jobs. Don't you make any more mistakes."

Charles laughed.

"All right, Baviera," said Kingsmill, "when I'm through talking you can answer me, then I want you to leave the radio on stand-by. Now, push the button."

The radio hissed and squawked, filling the limo with static. Then a droning voice said, "Okay, boss. I'll find her."

The static cut out, and Kingsmill stuffed the radio in a pocket on the back of the front seat. "We're all set."

"So it seems," said Charles.

The tracker kept on beeping. Keelor Ru was still making time, maintaining his lead, but Darma knew that wouldn't last. He'd stop somewhere and go right to the real bones, then they'd pounce on him. *More* killing.

Darma wondered if they would kill him, too. After all, they had Elliot to champion the fossils. And Elliot had the advantage of not knowing they were faked.

Darma moved even closer to the edge of the seat, but he could still feel the warmth of Kingsmill's body pressing against him. The man seemed to be leaning on him, harder and harder.

Keelor Ru was less than five klicks from the caves when his junker car started to die under him. First the grinding noises, riding up through the floorboards, making his head ache; then the hesitations, the small decelerations, as if a fitful wind was blowing the car around the road.

"Oh, no . . ."

The car slowed, lurched, and sped up.

"*Damn* it . . ."

He wrenched the steering wheel, throwing the car around a boulder. When he hit the accelerator, the car just *sat* there, coasting, then it took off with a scream, almost running him into a gully.

"Come on, you stupid . . . *stupid* . . ."

The car shimmied and bucked; the grinding noise got *loud*— and broke off. The car coasted to a dead stop, the smell of burned transmission oil seeped in.

Panel lights glowed red.

Keelor Ru turned off the ignition. There was no point in trying to get this piece of junk moving again. The tranny had gobbled itself up.

For a moment he just sat there, cursing Novas. Then he climbed out and looked around. The evening mist was fading, and the hard, steady sparks of the nighttime sky showed through the branches. This road was rarely traveled, though it led right to the caves.

Keelor started walking, noticed the headlights were still burning, and turned back to the car. It was then he saw there were fresh tracks in the dirt, tracks in front of his tires. Several vehicles had passed this way recently.

He looked up the road. Even this far away, and even in the dark, he could not make out the swelling lump that rose from the forest floor. That's where the tracks were headed, right for Maru'ka Ba Nos, the Sacred Mound.

Somebody was out there.

Somebody had beat him to it.

When Professor Digger was sure everybody had left the cell, he pushed the stone slab upward and let it slide to the floor. He climbed out silently and assisted Sylvie from the hole of compacted dirt.

She was rather filthy, her face and hair caked with mud and dirt, but she was glad to be out in the fresh air. She glanced back at the hole and whispered, "They don't call you Professor Digger for nothing."

"That would be dishonest, I'm sure. I would have dug a longer tunnel, but I didn't know which way to go. There are limits, you know? My power reserves—"

"Okay, you can shut up now."

Sylvie scanned the deserted cell, noting the door left half open, and said, "C'mon, let's get out of here before they come back."

There was no one in the corridor. "Which way shall we try?" asked the professor.

"How should *I* know? I was unconscious when they brought us here."

The robot stood in the middle of the corridor and listened. "There is a small noise source to your right."

"Good."

Sylvie started off to her left. They soon came to a branching, but this time the professor declared each direction equally safe— or equally hazardous. They went right, just for variety. There was another turning not far from there. Left.

Then right.

Then left again.

"This is stupid," said Sylvie, as they ran out of lighted corridors. The damned place just went on forever, one sandstone tunnel after another. This couldn't be the ruined temple she'd seen on the map.

"Here's the thing," she said. "We can go back into the light and try some of the other lines—or we can go off into the dark."

"Our captors are almost certainly searching for us in the lighted sections."

"Why do you say that?"

"It's easier."

They started off into the darkness. Professor Digger had a

flashlight built into his hand, but Sylvie was leery of broadcasting their approach. "I also see in the dark," said Digger. "Infrared."

It didn't seem to make much difference. In effect, they were lost. Though Digger could easily memorize their turns, he didn't know where they had started. He had built-in maps, but all they revealed was that they were probably wandering the uncharted catacombs beneath the Sacred Mound.

The deeper they went, the weirder it got. The walls closed in and the ceiling dropped. When Sylvie tested, she found the stone walls had given way to packed dirt.

"Stop," she said, finally. "It's getting stuffy in here."

"That may be. I have no environmental testing equipment mounted internally."

"You mean, I'm the canary on this trip. I could be breathing poison right this minute—and you wouldn't notice anything until I dropped."

"Correct."

Sylvie thought about it. "Then I guess we have to go back. I don't want to asphyxiate myself."

"You know best, miss."

They turned back.

"What's that?" asked Zeke.

They had found some tracks and followed them with a growing sense of doom. Then, suddenly, a break.

"It's the junker!" said Marty.

Zeke slowed the van and pulled up behind the car in the middle of the dirt road. He shut off the engine but kept the lights on. Nothing moved in the car, and there was no sound anywhere around.

"Very cautiously. . ." said Zeke, opening his door.

They all climbed out and looked the car over. The keys were still in the ignition.

"Look at this," said Marty, shining his light on the dirt behind the car. There was an irridescent trail leading away, as though the old gray car were a giant slug. Marty got some of the fluid in his hand and slid it between his fingertips. He smelled it, looking thoughtful, and smiled. "Man ate his transmission."

Zeke and Merrily climbed into the car and looked around, but there were no clues as to who had been driving.

Marty came back from his inspection of the road and stood beside the driver's window. "He left on foot."

"But that's perfect, isn't it?" said Merrily. "We should be able to catch him now."

"Just the opposite," said Zeke. "A man on foot could see and hear us coming in plenty of time to duck into the woods. If he's armed, we're really screwed."

Marty said, "One set of tracks, Doc."

"That's what I figured. I know Sylvie hasn't been in this car."

"How can you tell?" asked Merrily.

"I know her scent."

CHAPTER 26

At the next turning Digger stopped, his coppery head swiveling this way and that. "There seems to be a search on for us."

"Where?"

"Coming this way, I'm afraid. I can hear voices, and footsteps, and some metallic clanking noises."

"Bracelets?"

"Knives."

"Coming this way?" she asked, straining to see to the end of the dark corridor. "From where?"

"Turn to your right, Miss Pharr. Try cupping your hands to your ears."

She tried it, but there was nothing to hear but a distant thrumming noise. She turned her head, using the more sensitive parts of her eyes, trying not to look directly down the corridor. Something flickered.

Zeke and Marty and Merrily stood around by the abandoned car, wondering what to do next.

Doc said, "It would help to know how long this heap has been sitting here."

"I'll ask it," said Marty.

He got behind the wheel and turned the key to STAND BY. "Hello, car."

"Welcome aboard."

"What is your status?"

"Massive transmission failure."

"Please specify."

"The intermediate sprag is locked up, the forward clutch has seized, the output gear's shaft has suffered tooth loss, hydraulic pressure has exceeded manufacturer's recommended maximum, seals have blown, and consequently the hydraulic fluid level is now well below manufacturer's recommended minimum. Please exchange this transmission for another, as simple repairs are impossible."

"I see. When did this malfunction occur?"

"After three hundred fifty-seven thousand one hundred ninety-eight kilometer's operation."

Zeke said, "Somebody's been running the poor thing ragged."

"I know," said Marty. To the car he said, "I need to know the time of the malfunction."

"Eleven thousand nine hundred and—"

"Not since the beginning," said Marty. "How long since the malfunction?"

"Sixteen minutes and forty seconds . . . mark."

Zeke looked up the dark road. "He couldn't be far."

"He might be right out there," said Merrily. "Watching us."

Zeke looked at Marty. "She's right."

"Who was the driver?" Marty asked the car.

"Unregistered."

"Was it the owner?"

"My ownership status is void. My memory has been partially erased."

"How do you know that?"

"Security circuits cannot be erased without indicating total operational failure."

"Have the police been notified?"

"I don't know. Certain areas of memory have been altered."

"Has a tow service been notified of your malfunction?"

"I don't know. Certain areas of—"

"Thank you."

Marty turned to Doc. "Any ideas?"

"Yeah, ask the car where it was headed."

"Oh," said Marty. "Nice one."

He asked, and the car replied, "I am in manual control at this time. My destination is not known, though my position is."

"Nice try," said Marty.

"Wait a minute," said Doc. "Ask the car what it means, its position is known?"

"Okay." He did.

"I am broadcasting a beacon," said the car. "Upon request."

"What request?"

"Intermittent radio transmission prompts me to transmit the coordinate readout of my inertial guidance system."

"How often does that happen?"

"At random intervals, averaging every fifteen seconds."

"You're still doing it?"

"Yes."

Marty looked at Zeke. "Our guy has a tail."

Doc turned to stare back down the empty road. "Who would do that?"

"Beats me. Rebels?"

"Okay, let's assume our guy is going someplace—someplace secret and important. If he suspects somebody is after him—"

"He was sure driving like a guy in a hurry."

"—then he may still be trying to get there. He won't hide in the bushes as long as the road is clear."

"But we can't go after him," said Marty, "or he *will* hide."

"Well, we can't go on foot. He's got too much of a headstart."

Merrily said, "It's simple. Figure out how far he could get, drive nearly that far, then get out on foot and try to sneak up on him."

Zeke smiled. "That is almost perfect."

Keelor Ru trotted some more and fell back into a fast walk. His lungs were like hot stones in his chest, and he kept hacking up sour clumps of spit. He wasn't moving as fast as he had hoped.

He turned and looked down the road. Somewhere back there, mixed with the sound of his wheezing breath and pounding heart, was the faint hum of a motor. He cupped his hands behind his ears and held his breath. He could feel his heartbeat crashing into the back of his neck. He strained to hear—grabbed a fast breath —and tried again.

Yes . . . there it was . . . a growling noise . . . the whine of turbines . . . and *there*! the shifting glitter of headlights through the trees.

He started to run up the middle of the road.

The car kept on coming. Now he could hear it behind him, gobbling the ground between them. Faint light flickered at the tops of the trees in front of him.

Keelor Ru emitted a strangled, breathless scream and cut to the right, bounding through the bushes to the safety of the big trees. He got behind one and stopped, puffing loudly. He covered his mouth with his hands, trying to stifle the sound, but that only made it worse. He opened his mouth as wide as possible and took long, slow breaths.

For a moment he lost track of the car. His heart was beating so hard it felt like there was somebody behind him rapping the back of his head with a ball peen hammer. He wiped the sweat off his face and opened his eyes wide.

The car was still coming, its headlights throwing beams all over the road and the edge of the forest. Keelor ducked as the car rocketed past.

After a minute he crept from behind the tree.

Who would be out there on the road tonight? Was it really possible they were looking for him? Looking *here*? Did they already know that much? He thought about the car Novas had sold him. *Had* it been bugged?

Keelor Ru stepped back out on the road and looked up where the car had disappeared. It was gone, the road deserted. He started walking again.

In five minutes he stopped, listening. There was somebody on the road behind him, somebody on foot, walking up the road toward him.

He stood for a long moment, frozen in the middle of the road, heartbeat hissing in his ears.

Wait a minute. The footsteps had stopped. He strained to hear, but now there was nothing but his pounding heart. He took several steps and stopped. Still nothing. He began to doubt. Had there ever been footsteps behind him?

"Maybe I'm going nuts."

He started to walk again . . . and stopped. The footsteps were back. He waited. The footsteps continued, becoming distinct, becoming *real* . . .

He crouched and tried to see back down the road. Something moved. A tree? A person? Something moved in time with the faint crunching noise. Was somebody really there?

Keelor Ru started moving again, slowly at first, then faster . . . faster . . . jogging . . . running . . . running *hard* . . .

He wanted to stop and listen, to find out if the footsteps were coming faster too, but he didn't dare. He was running full out, in panic, desperately trying to put space between himself and the phantom footsteps, running as hard as he—

Keelor tripped, hitting the dirt road hard, crumpling up in pain. He started to rise . . . and found somebody sitting on his chest. Brilliant white light exploded in his face.

"It's Keelor Ru!" someone said.

"You're going to kill me!"

The man laughed. "Not exactly."

Running footsteps approached; the light shifted, and Keelor got his first look at the guy chasing him. He was a fat, silver-skinned dwarf.

"Nice work," the little guy said, carefully stepping over the trip wire that was stretched across the road.

The light shifted again, into Keelor's eyes. "Guess who this is," said the man sitting on his chest.

"He looks familiar," said the dwarf.

"He's the one who discovered the fossils."

"Who are you?" asked Keelor Ru.

"Ezekiel Bones," the man said. "And have I got some questions for you."

Escont and his men were searching the abandoned car. Kingsmill climbed out of the limo and wandered over to watch. Bart Charles stayed in the car and got Baviera on the radio. "Have you taken care of the woman yet?"

There was a long silence, and Charles had to repeat the question. "Answer me!"

"Almost."

"What the hell does *that* mean?"

"She's still kind of lost right now."

"Damn it, you idiot! Find her and kill her at once. That robot, too."

"I'm trying my best," said Baviera. "These people can move through stone."

"Nonsense," said Charles.

He told Baviera the subject of his ambush was now on foot. "Start your people moving this way, down the road. We'll squeeze him from this side."

The radio hissed and coughed. "Uh, sir, I can't . . . I got no . . . I mean, those fellas got no radio, so I can't—"

"Send somebody down there with a message, you idiot."

"Yes, sir." After a pause he added, "They really *can* move through solid rock."

Bart Charles threw the radio back into the holder. "Superstitious bastards," he muttered. "They *deserve* a war."

Dr. Darma sat quietly in the corner, not moving. Charles shook his head at the Garukan, thinking, they're all the same.

"He's on foot," said Kingsmill, climbing back into the limo.

"I know that! Let's get going."

"But he'll hide when he sees—"

"We'll give him room," Charles said impatiently. "Besides, he's almost there."

"But we don't know where he's going."

"I think it's pretty obvious by now," said Charles. He gestured, and Kingsmill looked through the windshield.

Looming pale and ghost-like in the distant night sky was the Sacred Mound.

CHAPTER 27

Baviera's ambush team had got the word their quarry was now on foot. They were creeping down the deserted road when they saw the car coming. Confused, they dived for the bushes. The car passed. It was a large camping van, its fat tires throwing gravel high into the air. Thirty seconds later there was nothing left but a pall of floating dust.

The ambush team sat down on the ground and waited for the runner to find Baviera and get instructions.

One of the Rzar rubbed some of the green paint off his jutting cheekbones. "I don't know about you," he said to his companion, "but I'm not getting enough money for this shit."

Keelor Ru sat up front in the van. About five minutes after they passed the Rzar natives, Ru suddenly pointed. "Go right!"

"*Damn* it!" said Zeke, hitting the brakes. The van fishtailed all over the road, its tires digging into the loose dirt. "Gimme more warning, next time." He backed up, using the spotlight to find the turn. "This's only a trail."

"It's a shortcut to the base of the Mound," said Ru.

"So scratch the paint a little," said Marty. "It's just a rental."

"That's a lousy attitude," said Zeke, putting the van into forward gear. After a moment, the trail widened out. "You know, this may work."

"There are many entrances to the catacombs," said the Garukan. "I have to go in the right one, or I don't think I could find the bones."

Zeke asked him if he knew how the other bones were faked. Keelor Ru said they never told him, but he knew his were genuine.

"It just worries me that you got away with them," said Zeke. "If they are what you say, I would have expected Darma to destroy them at once."

Keelor nodded. "He came to me after he found out what they wanted to do. He said we should take their money, but that we should hide the bones, not destroy them, as they asked. I really think Darma was impressed by the fossils. He respects the past."

"I'll bet!" said Marty.

"It's true," said Keelor. "All the time I've known him he's dreamed of finding the real thing. Then those men came, corrupting him with their money and their threats. I was afraid he'd crack and give back the bones, so I stole them and ran away."

"You didn't get very far," said Marty.

Ru hesitated. "I guess I couldn't leave the bones."

"Some people up there in the road," said the driver, slowing down. The limo was in the lead now, having beaten the guncar away from Keelor Ru's abandoned hulk.

Bart Charles leaned forward. Half a dozen painted Garukans stood up in the glare of the limo's headlights, looking confused.

"Those are Baviera's men," said Kingsmill. "Rzar natives."

"Sir?" said the driver. "What should I do?"

Kingsmill said to Charles, "He must have gotten by them."

"Or he got off the road and we've passed him."

"Sir?" said the driver.

"Go," Charles told him. "Drive straight to the Mound."

"Yes, sir."

The limo sped up, the guncar right on its tail.

"What if he's not there?" said Kingsmill.

"He'll be there," said Charles, "because that's where he's hidden the bones. That much is obvious now. We may not even need him."

"But without Keelor Ru, we haven't a chance in hell of finding those bones. The catacombs run all through—"

"We don't need to find the bones," said Charles. "All we have to do is destroy them." He turned to Dr. Darma. "You know these people."

"I am one of them," said Darma.

There was in his voice a goofy sort of pride that made Bart Charles smile. "Yeah, right—so you should know, Darma. What sort of war could we get if the Sacred Mound were nuked from orbit?"

"Kill the engine!" said Keelor Ru.

Zeke complied, and the van rolled to a stop behind the last of the trees. Everybody climbed down and moved cautiously forward. Almost immediately the trees gave out, and they stepped into a clearing. Directly in front of them, rising fifteen hundred meters into the black sky, carving its shape from the background of stars, was the Sacred Mound. Overhead, stretched out along the top of the Mound like some kind of jealous guardian, was Ursa Major, hardly distorted by the shift from one star system to another.

Marty whistled.

Zeke held up the nightscope and inspected the base of the Mound. It was crowded with the statues of demons and gods caught in dramatic poses. Beneath ornate arches bird- and lizard-headed men cavorted in ceremonial dress, while others, outfitted with crude armor, clashed in battle on a vast scale. "Keelor, you say this is all one rock, carved by hand?"

"Correct."

"What about the catacombs?"

"Yes, yes, carved by hand over thousands of years. Most were cut from living sandstone, the rest burrowed through dirt and packed hard. Kilometer after kilometer."

Marty said, "Hell of a place to hide something."

"I know just where to go," said Keelor Ru, stepping forward.

Doc hung back.

"What's the matter?" asked Merrily.

"Finding the bones will be nice," he said. "But what the hell happened to Sylvie and Professor Digger?"

"What's this?" asked Sylvie, moving closer to a large lump that oozed from the mud. This part of the catacombs was so very dark and slippery Sylvie insisted Digger project a dim light, which reflected off the slimy walls.

"Pardon me?" whispered Professor Digger. He had put his hearing on maximum, and kept his head in a constant scan. He didn't so much appear vigilant as *ditsy.* "What's what?"

"This thing," said Sylvie, reaching out. She pried at the mud until a mottled Garukan skull emerged.

She screamed, then clamped a hand over her mouth. Digger's head began to swivel twice as fast.

"I'm clocking the echoes," he said.

"Sorry," she whispered, staring at the skull.

Even in the dim light she could see it was moving, forced by hydrostatic pressure from the wet mud. Now it seemed the whole skeleton was sliding from the wall in slow motion. Beside it was another one, coming out. Sylvie's eyes grew large, and a tiny squeak slipped from between her lips.

"Ancient citizens of Garu'ka," said Professor Digger. "I would estimate several thousand years old."

"The Sacred Mound," said Sylvie, eyes widening further. "It's a *burial* mound!"

"Of course, what did you think?" said Digger. "Maru'ka Ba Nos: the House of the Dead."

Sylvie backed up, colliding with another muddy stack of bones. Oh God, the corridor ahead was *crowded* with them. "They're everywhere . . ." she said in a faint, high-pitched voice. "Let's go back the other way, toward the light."

"Impossible," said Professor Digger. "They heard your scream. And they're coming this way."

He grabbed her hand and dragged her into the darkness. Hard, wet things brushed against her.

"Stop moaning," said Digger.

"Go to hell!"

For that he made her run. Slimy bones seemed to reach from the walls, snatching at her arms. Her moan rolled up into a scream. Then the corridor squeezed down to a dead end.

"Funny," said the professor. "That never happened before."

Baviera grinned. "Hear that scream? I think we got her cornered."

The search party began to run. Extra knives appeared from their sheaths, ready for action. *Finally.*

The deserted cave entrance was hidden by brush. "You're sure this is it?" asked Zeke, as he watched Keelor Ru pry the branches aside.

"Positive," he said, shining the light around in there. "Come on."

Marty followed, then Merrily, then Doc. The walls were lined with stone blocks, their seams plastered with mud. "How far is it?" asked Zeke.

"Not far," said Keelor, walking quickly.

"Is it a good hiding spot?" asked Marty.

Keelor turned, his light shifting shadows all across the walls. "Wait till you see."

• • •

Sylvie was gagging on the mud that flew into her face. She tried to yell, got a bitter mouthful, and shut up fast. Professor Digger's churning hands maintained a hurried pace, drilling their cramped tunnel through the soft mud. Occasionally something heavy would smack her face—more ancient bones.

Sylvie wanted to scream, but there was no point. The tunnel pressed in, drooping overhead. If she could have gotten out the way they came in, she might have tried it, but the professor had dropped the roof, sealing them inside.

On he went, digging and squirming, compressing the mud to the sides of the tunnel. In front she could hear the exaggerated whine of his motored muscles, from behind came the muffled sound of their pursuers, digging after them.

She felt trapped, could sense the whole enormous weight of the Sacred Mound pressing down. Her hand closed on a leg bone, which she tossed behind her with a groan. She ducked her head and shielded her mouth from the flying mud. "Hurry up!"

"I am operating at maximum power demand," said the robot, his voice muffled. "If this were not exceptionally easy going, I suspect I might have burned out some time ago."

Sylvie felt another scream coming. If Digger drained his power pack, they'd be trapped in there.

"Oh, Miss Pharr," he said, his voice infuriatingly calm, "I think I may have some good news very soon. Yes, yes, I really think . . . I think . . . I think . . ."

His voice trailed off, as if the robot were getting drowsy. Sylvie listened to the sounds of his digging hands. Oh, God, he was slowing down, he really *was*.

CHAPTER 28

Two of Baviera's natives guarded the Mound's main entrance. Kingsmill knew a little of the language, and he tried to get the Garukans to take them to their boss. The guards seemed not to understand. Kingsmill turned away. "Can you help us, Colonel Escont?"

"Sorry, the Rzar speak a strange dialect. They refuse to learn standard. Try again."

Kingsmill did, but the guards just laughed. Bart Charles was about to go nuts.

"Come *on!*" he said, moving forward. "We don't have time to—"

The guards stopped laughing and whipped out long swords. They stood their ground. Charles stepped back, his face growing dark with anger. "Take 'em out," he told the gunmen.

"Wait!" said Kingsmill. "Where the hell is Darma?"

Escont went back to the limo and found the doctor still in the backseat. "They need you to talk to the natives."

Darma looked up, his eyes bleary. "Why don't you just kill them? That's what you people do best."

Escont snarled and jerked Darma out of the car. "Don't give me any trouble." He marched the squirming doctor to the cave entrance.

"Nice of you to join us," said Bart Charles. "Call these animals off . . . before we burn holes in them."

Darma spoke the local dialect. "You men must let these monsters pass into Maru'ka Ba Nos. One of you lead them to Baviera."

The guards discussed it, then one of them asked, "Why are they so stupid?"

"Bad genes," said Darma.

They followed Keelor Ru through a bewildering series of turns. "I hope you know what you're doing," said Zeke.

"I memorized the route," said the Garukan.

The cave walls were surfaced in pebbly white stone, alternately smooth and rough, as if the carving had never been completed. Sometimes they entered vaults where ceilings all but disappeared into the darkness above them, raining water as if from the open sky. Other times the tunnel squeezed down, the ceiling so low they had to crawl.

Marty was chewing on a candy bar. From time to time he dropped a tiny piece of wrapper, just to mark the trail. Not that he didn't trust the Garukan, but what if something should happen to him? Better safe than sorry.

Baviera's radio kept squawking.

"I'm coming!" he yelled, his voice echoing through the catacombs. Gad, that Kingsmill was an insistent geek!

Manel was encrusted with drying mud, but there was no time to clean up. One of the Rzar came with him to find the boss; the others stayed behind to make sure nobody stopped digging. The girl and the stupid robot were trapped in a hole of their own making. It was a strange business, and it made the Rzar nervous.

The native with Baviera mumbled to himself, and bent to pick up something shiny and colorful. He chirped happily and put it in his hair.

Idiot, thought Baviera.

They were almost to the main chamber, where the boss was waiting, when the native sang a happy note and reached to pick up another bit of shiny junk.

"What the hell are you doing?" asked Manel.

"They're mine!" said the Rzar, edging away. He stuck the new piece in his hair opposite the first.

Baviera cursed and trained his light on it. Shiny paper, silver and red, with some sort of writing on it. As the native bent to grab another piece, Manel snatched the paper out of his hair.

"Hey!" said the native, whirling around.

Baviera cursed again and pushed him around the next corner, up the corridor, and into the main chamber.

"About time," said Kingsmill, coming up. "What's that?"

Baviera showed him the paper.

"Where'd this come from?"

Manel jerked his thumb at the Rzar, who was fading fast into the background. "He picked it up off the ground. He has more of them."

It took the colonel and two of the gunmen to get the rest of the paper from the screaming native. Kingsmill arranged the pieces on a flat stone.

"'Hershey's,'" said Escont.

"Bones is here," said Bart Charles.

It was a corridor of bones.

Zeke pointed his red-filtered flashlight in all directions, trying to see everything. He couldn't stop grinning. "There's thousands of them!"

The corridor was narrow, its sides cut into rough shelves, making four tiers of grisly display. The bones—crosshatched piles of ribs, arm and leg bones, with a jawless skull on top—were clean and old. They had obviously been laid out like this in ceremony.

Keelor Ru hurried through the corridor, hardly glancing back when Zeke tugged at his billowing shirt. "Wait a minute! Tell me about these bones!"

"As you see," said Ru. "My primitive ancestors used to put their dead on display—but not for hundreds of years."

Zeke dawdled, wanting to examine each set. Marty tried to shove him along, and Merrily began to whine. "It's *icky* in here."

The corridor narrowed further, and the headway dropped until only Marty, bringing up the rear, was comfortable walking upright. The display shelves down this way were obviously older: crude and crumbling, with bones scattered on the hardpacked dirt floor, having tumbled from their perch of honor.

"The deeper we go, the older the bones," said Keelor Ru. "New burials force the old ones along, until finally. . ."

"Finally what?" asked Bones, bent nearly double.

Marty shushed him. "Everybody *stop!*" he hissed.

They stopped, balanced on the crunchy, brittle bones.

Footsteps approached, moving fast.

Zeke killed his red light and turned. White light flickered behind them. And voices. Lots of angry voices.

"There they are!" yelled Bart Charles, rushing forward. Up ahead, in the squeezed-down end of the corridor of bones, he could see Zeke and Marty and Keelor Ru digging frantically at the muddy roof and sides, clawing away with ancient thighbones, filling the passageway with dirt, sealing themselves off.

Good. Excellent.

Kingsmill ran up as the fugitives disappeared. "Is it them?"

"Who the hell do you think?"

• • •

They dug like crazy, tearing at the soft dirt. "Keep going!" said Zeke. "Make 'em work for it!"

Marty stopped to examine the roof. "Gimme a hand here!"

Zeke swung his light around, and a hundred black shadows shifted in a hundred redlit eye sockets. Skulls lined the walls, oozing from the mud, the remnants of ever more primitive burial.

Marty was prying with his big screwdriver at a smooth bracing stone that capped uprights half buried in the sides of the tunnel. Zeke pitched in with a thighbone. Together they dug loose one end of the capping stone, then jumped back as the roof collapsed.

"That'll hold 'em," Marty said, wiping his hands.

Zeke turned, his light flashing past the grinning, faceless faces in the walls. The first living face he saw looked dead, gone white with panic. "Merrily," he said. "Don't worry, we'll get out of this."

She stared into his eyes, as if afraid to see the hundred empty eyes that watched them from the walls. Beyond her Keelor Ru waited, kneeling in the tunnel. "We're almost there," he said. "You ready?"

Zeke nodded. The Garukan turned, crawled a few meters, and dropped out of sight.

"Where'd he go?" asked Marty.

They followed.

Without warning the skull-lined tunnel dropped off into a tall rounded chamber. Zeke shined his red-filtered light around, breathless with horrible fascination. "Don't let Merrily see this," he whispered to Marty, who crouched like a plug in the tunnel's mouth.

The chamber was a wall-to-wall jumble of bones—skulls, thighs, ribs and spines—a vast pit of wet, discolored bones, the mottled remains of thousands of individuals tangled in death.

Across the way, perched atop the pile and grinning like a maniac, sat Keelor Ru. "You like it? You *must* like it, a man named Bones. You *must!*"

Zeke flashed a grin, and turned his light to white.

"Don't do that!" screamed Keelor Ru, throwing an arm over his eyes.

"Why not?" asked Zeke, going back to red. "They already know we're here."

"Not for them," said Keelor Ru. "For me. I need my dark-adapted eyes to find the fossils."

"They're here?" said Bones, his eyes darting about. "Where?"

"Everywhere. Turn out your light."

Zeke hesitated, then looked back at Marty. "Try to keep Merrily from screaming. It's gonna get dark."

He turned off his light and waited. The pit of bones seemed to jump up at him in his mind, and behind him Merrily whimpered as Marty talked some soothing nonsense.

Abruptly the room was back, defined by points of throbbing blue light. For a moment he was dizzy and disoriented. He turned and turned again, feeling helpless. Then a pale blue skull floated in front of his face. He nearly screamed. The skull began to dance in midair, as someone laughed and the bone pile crackled and snapped.

Professor Digger moved slower and slower. His leg and arm muscles whined and growled, filling the horrible tunnel with acrid ozone. His light was off now, and the close, wet darkness was like a grave waiting to become official.

Sylvie could hear the dull thump and scrape of the natives digging behind her, getting closer all the time. Damn, what a *filthy* way to die.

The professor was trying to say something, but couldn't seem to figure out what words to say or how to say them.

"Come on," she said, pushing at Digger's strange feet.

"Uh . . . uh . . . uh . . . ," he said, his voice low and distorted.

"Come on, you stupid hunk of—"

At that moment someone grabbed her ankle and she just *had* to scream.

Throughout the dark cavern the giggling Garukan scrabbled, gathering up the scattered bones. Like magic the glowing blue chunks lifted and flew and dived to land in a growing pile in Keelor Ru's spread-out shirt.

"You coated them," said Zeke, grinning at the airborne bones. "What do you have—"

"Ultraviolet projector," said Ru. All around the room bones flared brightly then went dim as the beam passed. "I wanted to hide the fossils where they would not be noticed. So I figured, in a room full of bones . . ."

"It worked," said Zeke, moving across the bone heap toward the glowing pile. "Let me just see what—"

"Bones!" said Marty. "They're coming! I can hear them digging!"

"Damn it!" said Bones, then, to Keelor Ru, "The light!"

The cave darkened, the bones fading fast as the fluorescent paint gave up the energy it had absorbed. They waited in the dark and listened to the frantic digging.

"Wait a minute . . ." said Bones. "Am I turned around or is that not coming from—"

"Bones!" yelled Marty.

A weak beam of yellow light pierced the cave wall, about halfway up. Someone was struggling up there, kicking, yelling, digging, pushing, cursing.

"I know that voice," said Bones.

Sylvie kicked at the hands behind her, then drove her boots into the ceiling of the tunnel, collapsing the soft dirt. Someone complained in a muffled voice. She kicked again, and more dirt came down.

"Get going!" she yelled at Digger.

His muscles whined, moved fitfully, and slowed again.

"Damn it!" she said, squeezing past him. "*I'll* dig!"

Her fingers thrust out, clawing at the face of the cut—and broke free, into the open. "You idiot! All this time we were almost through!"

She banged Digger on his head, and it lit up with feeble yellow light. "You still have *some* power." She could hear the natives tearing through her impromptu cave-in, coming hard and fast. "All right, Digger, listen to me, you hunk of steaming junk, I know you're holding back on me. You guys always do. Okay, now I want it. Emergency release. Maximum human danger. Self-preservation override. You hear me? Dump your reserves. I want your last erg, buddy. Your life for mine, you hear me? Stop . . . those . . . guys!"

The robot jerked to life, his head glowing brightly, and began to slice the tunnel's roof. Dirt thudded into place, blocking the way.

Sylvie clawed more of the opening, then spat dirt out of her mouth. Unexpectedly the air felt cool and she fell flat on her stomach in the darkness, sliding face first along an endless pile of bones. "Oh, my God . . ."

"Stop complaining," someone said, and she thought, I know that voice. . . .

CHAPTER 29

Charles looked at Dr. Darma. "You should have destroyed the bones when I told you to."

Darma muttered something about their being priceless.

"I beg your pardon?" said Charles. "Priceless, did you say? There's *nothing* I can't put a price on—and to me the bones are worth more destroyed."

Darma didn't answer.

Charles went on. "But then I'm not pretending to be some hotshot scientist."

Baviera popped out of the muddy, skull-lined tunnel. "The roof's collapsed. It's gonna take a while."

"Tell me again where you left the robot and the black-haired girl?" said Charles.

Baviera did.

"All right," said Charles, "call your people back. Tell them to seal up that tunnel." He turned to Kingsmill. "As I see it, they're all in about the same area, and the robot's digging to intersect. By now they may even have found each other—and figured out it's hopeless."

He sent one of his men back to the guncar for explosives. He wouldn't need to nuke the Mound from space after all.

Zeke was oblivious to everything but Keelor Ru's fossils. He sat cross-legged in the ancient ossuary and made a rough assemblage of the brown, breccia-coated skull pieces. It was humanoid, about the size of a *Homo erectus*, but with the distinctive Garukan cheekbones already well developed. "If this tests out . . ."

"The ground was undisturbed," said Keelor Ru. "I swear. And several guards saw me find it."

Zeke nodded. He wasn't worried about provenance right now. He arranged the bones in a skeletal shape, leaving space for the missing pieces—they would probably never be found now. "Look at the way the thigh bone attaches to the knee. See the angle? It bends inward from the pelvis."

"I know," said Ru. "This creature walked upright."

"Hey, Bones," said Marty. "I think they stopped digging out there."

"Whatever." Zeke examined the shoulder bones. "Look at these holes here."

"Muscle attachment places," said Keelor Ru.

"Oversized," said Zeke. "That could mean wings."

"Garu'ka is littered with the bones of ancient birds," said Keelor.

Zeke looked up at him and grinned. "I know."

"Bones?" said Marty. "Listen to me. They're up to something out there."

Zeke nodded impatiently. To Keelor Ru he said, "I've always thought you Garukans descended from large, flightless birds. Let's look at the feet."

There wasn't much to go on, and Zeke saw right away there would be some difficulty here. But as far as he was concerned the bones of the feet showed definite signs of keratoid development. Claws? Probably.

"I like it," he said, grinning. "I like it . . . I really think we've got a live one here. If I can get this evidence in front of the right people, there can be no doubt. Earth will *have* to back off."

"You think so?" said Ru.

"Absolutely. With these bones you have the force of moral right. Public opinion will bury the reactionaries. The Galactic Council will have to step in. I have no doubt."

"The rebels—"

"Will have to be patient. It won't take long, and they won't have to fire a shot—but they'll have to be patient. They'll have to—"

"Hey!" yelled Sylvie. "Stop messing around with those stupid bones!"

Zeke looked up. "This is important!"

"So is dying," said Marty.

The man was back with the explosives. Charles set him to placing the main charges around the entrance of the corridor of bones. The concussion would knock 'em out, and the collapse of the tunnel's roof would seal them off forever. Not a bad deal.

Charles turned to Darma. "Go in there and tell your people to get out. I'm going to blow the access tunnel to keep them from getting to the main charges."

Darma was shocked. "But this is a sacred site. You can't just—"

"Get in there, I said, or I'll blow the place with the natives inside. Maybe they'd consider it an honor to be buried with their ancestors."

Darma didn't move. "If they knew what those bones proved, they'd kill you."

Charles laughed. "But you won't tell them. For your part in this, they'd tear you to pieces."

"It might be worth it," said Darma.

Bart Charles moved toward him. He was not a young man, but the aura of physical power was unmistakable. Darma backed up. "Get in there and tell them," said Charles. Darma obeyed.

Charles smiled. "Take a shovel," he told one of his gunmen. "When he sticks his head out again, bop him." He looked at Kingsmill. "I think we're through with Dr. Darma, don't you?"

Kingsmill turned away.

But Colonel Escont was grinning. He looked as if he wanted to swing the shovel himself.

"If they use explosives," said Marty, "they can drop the roof on us. The soil here is not very stable."

"What are we going to do?" asked Sylvie. "Can we dig our way out?"

"Which way?" asked Marty. "Besides, our only real chance is Professor Digger—the piece of junk—and he's conked out."

The professor made no protest, but leaned against the wall, his headlight fading out. As Sylvie had insisted, he'd given his life.

"We need something to build with," said Marty, looking around. "Something we can use to reinforce the roof."

Sylvie glanced about with a sneer. "All we've got is bones."

Marty stared at her a moment, then reached into his jacket, pulling out a fat tube of Rodale's Superglue. "I wonder if this stuff works on bones?"

Bart Charles leaned over the bundle of explosive packs. "The main charges are set to go," he told Kingsmill, "soon as I tap the timer. After that we've got twenty minutes." He grabbed one of the grenades, then hesitated with his finger on the start button. "Are you ready?"

Kingsmill watched the tunnel entrance, looking scared. "We shouldn't do this."

Charles tapped the button anyway and the timer began to clock down. He stood up, flicking the safety off a grenade. He waved it at Kingsmill, then tossed it into the tunnel of bones, past the unconscious body of Dr. Darma. He walked quickly away, passing Kingsmill. "Perhaps you'd rather stay."

Kingsmill turned, looking disoriented. "It never stops, does it? Once you start killing . . ."

"Come on."

Kingsmill stumbled forward, and Bart yanked him around the next corner. The grenade went off with a *thump*, and the corridor filled with bone dust.

"Merrily . . ."

"Don't worry," said Charles. "She'll never find out."

They strode through the tunnels. Time was running out.

In just a few minutes the five of them, working furiously, dug through the accumulated bones and cleared a hollow. The bones kept sliding back down, trying to fill in the hole, so Merrily and Sylvie went around the outside of the cleared zone, tossing everything back but thighbones and tibias. Marty was in charge of shelter design.

"I'd like to build a geodesic dome," he said. "They're lightweight and strong and everything—but all we got to work with are femurs and tibias. The only two-strut dome I know—it's called a 2-frequency icosa alternate—would be too small. See, the size of the femur determines the overall diameter of the dome. With these Garukan bones we'd get a dome about two meters across. And that's just a bit too cramped, even for good friends."

"So build two of them," said Zeke.

"What, and be responsible for deciding who goes in which dome? What if one of them gets squashed like a ripe mellon? I don't want that on my head."

"Okay, no mellon on your head," said Sylvie. "What are you going to do?"

"And *when* are you going to do it?" asked Merrily. "I thought we were in a hurry."

"We are," said Marty. "But time spent on good, sound planning is never wasted—unless the bomb goes off in the next few seconds."

"What are you going to *do*?" asked Zeke, becoming impatient.

"I have no choice," said Marty. "I'll have to build two domes."

"But you said—"

"Stuck bottom to bottom," said Marty. "A sphere, in other words."

Zeke agreed—anything to get started—and Marty explained the design. Each hemisphere consisted of a pentagon surrounded by five more pentagons, touching at the corners. The pentagons would be made from femurs, with tibias pointing inward to the centers for support. The faces of the pentagons would be a little flat—the tibias were a tad short—but that couldn't be helped.

"All right, let's go," said Marty.

First they laid out the bottom pentagon and glued it together. Bracing struts were omitted. Next they used it as a template to make five more pentagons, each braced with tibias. Then five more, this time omitting one outside femur edge.

"Now we assemble it," said Marty.

The bottom course of complete pentagons went down on their points, at the junctures of the bones of the bottom plate.

"Lean 'em back," said Marty, "until the elbows touch."

Merrily grumbled to Sylvie. "I thought these were *leg* bones."

"I heard that," said Marty. "I mean the middle corners."

"I know," she said.

Rodale's Superglue set ultra fast, and only a few drops were needed at each junction. As the inverted dome went up, the pieces locked together.

"Now," said Marty, "we need femur struts across the top, filling out the equator."

The open-ended pentagons came next, the open side lined up on top of the those of the bottom course, again glued at the elbows—this time leaning inward.

"Almost done," said Marty.

More femur struts were needed to close the top, forming the last pentagon. By this time everybody was inside the sphere but Marty, who was perched on the sliding, clattering slope of the bone pile. "How many femurs you got left?"

"Two," said Zeke, lining them up, both from the right leg, too. They looked identical.

"Two?" said Marty. "Oh, no, we're short three femurs!"

He turned and pawed through the bone pile, rejecting arm bones left and right. "Come on, come *on*! There *has* to be more than—*ah*!"

Found one.

He threw the bone to Zeke, who stood with his head poking out of the top of the sphere. Marty dived back into the pile, tossing bones over his shoulder, *clack, click, clack*.

"Maybe you'd better forget about it," said Zeke. "This'll be all right."

"It'll collapse!" said Marty, his voice muffled. He was buried to his waist in bones, headfirst. He surfaced abruptly, screaming a curse. "That *can't* be all the thighbones in here!"

Keelor Ru sat inside the sphere, cradling something in his lap. He kept his mouth shut.

"Get inside," Zeke told Marty. "It's been quiet out there for twenty minutes. If they set explosives—"

"Found one!" yelled the dwarf, holding the bone aloft in triumph. He tossed it to Zeke. "One more!"

"Get down here!" said Bones. "There isn't time!"

"No!"

"Look," said Sylvie. "We got plenty of tibias."

"They won't work!"

"Come on!" said Zeke.

Marty skidded down the noisy slope. "One more! One stinking thighbone, that's all I want. Just *one*! Just—" He stopped and looked in at Keelor Ru. "Wait a minute. I know where we can get another thighbone."

"No you don't!" yelled Ru.

"Come on, pal," said Marty. "Gimme!"

Keelor Ru hunkered down over his cache of fossil bones. "They're too valuable!"

"Oh, yeah?"

"Leave him alone," said Zeke. "His bones are too fragile."

"But we need one more," Marty whined.

"Use the tibias," said Zeke. "Splice 'em together. They'll fit if you overlap 'em."

"Are you kidding me?" said Marty. "That's shearing force. What do you want from Mr. Rodale, a miracle?"

"Do it!" said Zeke, in just the right tone of voice: a cross between *please* and *I'll kill you if you don't*.

Marty looked sick. He slid down the pile, kicking his big feet and whining like a kid. "Under protest," he said. "And I *won't* be responsible."

"Fine," said Zeke.

Marty glued the smaller bones together—grumbling all the while—then started to cave the contents of the ossuary onto the sphere, closing it in. Skulls rolled down, filling the chinks—except for the few that slipped through the bone mesh, dropping on the folks below.

"Stop it!" yelled Merrily. "Enough is enough, already! I don't need a bunch of old skulls in my lap!"

"Get down here, Marty!" said Zeke.

"Almost through . . ."

Charles waited out by the limo, staring at his watch. ". . . three . . . two . . . one . . ." The explosion came right on time, echoing through the Sacred Mound. The natives had all scattered by that time, so the only folks there to appreciate the situation were Kingsmill and one of the gunmen.

"The last of Ezekiel Bones," said Charles. He was grinning fiercely. All of the old debts were paid.

As if on cue, a great cloud of black dust came boiling out of the cave entrance. Charles kept on smiling. Ashes to ashes, dust to dust. How do you like it, Dr. Bones?

CHAPTER 30

Marty had no sooner shimmied inside the sphere, pulling the rest of the bonestack down on top of them, when the explosion went off. The sphere sagged as tons of dirt and rock landed on it. The top pentagon dropped half a meter with a loud creaking sound, pressing the already crowded folks even closer together. Bones snapped all around them, but most held, and the tangled nest beneath them absorbed the rest of the energy. The squashed sphere quivered under the load, as dirt poured down from a hundred leaks.

Merrily said, "I bit my tongue."

"Good," somebody said.

Another half minute passed; the roof of thighbones groaned and crackled ominously. But that was it.

"Oh, great," said Sylvie. "We survived the explosion. Now we can all look forward to suffocation. Anybody want to sing songs?"

"I'm amazed," said Marty, inspecting the spliced tibias with his flashlight. "Rodale's Superglue really came through."

"If we get out of here," said Zeke, "I'll buy the company."

"What do you mean *if*?"

"I feel a draft," said Merrily.

"God," said Marty, "all she ever does is complain."

"Wait a minute," said Zeke, his light shifting around. "A draft? Do you suppose . . ."

"Get that light out of my eyes," said Merrily.

Zeke grabbed a handful of bone dust and let it fall. Merrily sneezed.

Marty watched the floating dust and pointed. "That way." He squeezed out between the converging tibias on one of the bottom pentagons. Digging through the loose bones, he crawled off in the direction of the draft, until all they could see of him was his wide boot soles and his dusty butt. "Something happened here."

He began tossing bones and dirt back into the dome. There came a soft noise—*crump*—and more dust blew in from the small tunnel he'd built.

"Hey, cut it out!" said Merrily.

Marty crawled backwards into the dome, looking even dirtier than before, if possible. "We got an opening here. The roof's still coming down, but we got an opening. The explosion must have blown it out. There's a big room or something."

"Let's start digging," said Zeke. "It's getting a little close in here."

The new chamber was seventy or eighty meters across, too big for their flashlights to reveal. It looked almost perfectly spherical, the walls glossy and smooth. Their opening was a third of the way up the slope.

"What the hell could have made this?" asked Marty.

Zeke reached out and plucked a piece of shattered metal from the wall. "This place is full of junk." He handed the twisted piece of metal to Marty, then shined his light into the chamber. "Honest to God, there's junk everywhere."

He slid down the slope, using the imbedded metal scraps like ladder rungs. "Come on down," he called out over his shoulder. Pointless: they were already on the way.

At the bottom of the slope, in the bowl of the chamber, there was a lot more junk—fist-sized pieces of metal and plastic and ceramic. Some were painted, some were polished, most were green with corrosion and pitted clear through.

Bones kicked at the junk, and the clinking sound echoed through the chamber. Marty came up beside him. "Nothing natural could have made this."

"That's what I've been thinking."

"I wish I had my cameras," said Sylvie.

"I'm gonna set off a radio beacon," said Marty, pulling one out of his jacket.

"In here?" asked Zeke. "Do you think it would do any good?"

"Never can tell."

He reared back and flung the little yellow servo at the top of the chamber. Anchor barbs stuck in the ceiling, and the beacon began to flash red.

Zeke shrugged. "If it makes you happy."

• • •

Kadak!xa's sensors locked onto the beacon in three-fifths of a second. "Captain, we got a marker. I'm going down." Two seconds later she was off the bridge, rolling for the lander. "'Bout time," she muttered, mouthparts clicking.

Zeke reached into the pile of junk at his feet and picked up something he recognized. "I don't believe it . . ." He turned the piece of smooth plastic over in his fingers. It was heavy and dark, like the stuff they used to make ship's console edges. "You know what this is, all this junk? It's a ship, a spaceship. A spaceship crashed here."

"A spaceship?" said Marty. "This stuff looks about a million years old."

"Even so," said Zeke, playing with the piece of plastic. He rubbed at some scratches in the surface, then spat to loosen the dirt.

Sylvie came over to see. "This is part of a spaceship?"

Marty went kicking through the junk. "You know, this does look familiar, sort of. Like this piece . . . could be part of a fuel pump . . . or something . . ."

Zeke rubbed the plastic. Out of the muck letters were forming. "There's writing on this piece."

"Where?" said Sylvie. "Here, let me hold the light."

Bones buffed the letters. "This is . . . Roman script and some numerals . . ."

"You're right," said Sylvie. "It says, 'B . . . E . . . C.'"

Bones laughed, but he felt weird. Merrily came over and looked. "'1 . . . 3 . . . 5 . . . 7 . . . 5 . . . 0 . . . 5'" she said.

Zeke looked at Merrily and back at the plastic and then over at Sylvie. "I know this ship. I don't believe this, but it has to be. It's the *Dostoyevsky* . . . a BEC ship, reported missing three years ago. The insurance company just paid off."

"Nonsense," said Marty. "This ship is about a million years old. Look at it!"

"I *am* looking at it," said Bones. "It *is* a million years old. A million two hundred thousand, to be exact."

"What are you saying?" asked Sylvie. "They aged the bones in this thing?"

"Exactly," said Zeke. "And they used the IO to get it back."

"You believe that?" asked Marty.

"Nope," said Bones. He tossed the hunk of plastic to Merrily. "Here, kid. Don't believe everything you read."

Marty got pissed. "What are you saying now? That they *didn't* age the bones in this thing?"

"Oh, they did," said Bones. "They must have. They had this ship—stolen or whatever—and they put their fresh bones inside and sent it out there to wait a million years, just hoping the damned thing would work."

"Well, it did," said Marty, looking around. "Obviously, it worked."

Bones shook his head. "I still don't believe it. Someone would have found the ship. A million years, it was out there. Longer. And whatever looping trip they sent it on—out of the plane of the galaxy or whatever—it had to end up pretty close by. Stars in this region move less than eight hundred light-years in the time we're talking about. And what about the IO? My God, the IO was only invented thirty-four years ago. The way some folks talk, it's still experimental. Do you really expect the thing to sit out there for a million years and work perfectly?"

"But it *did*, Bones," said Sylvie. "Face it. If it did, it did."

Zeke pointed up at the spherical cavern. "What about this place? Marty says nothing natural could have done it. He's right. I think the crash must have jarred the IO. It came on for a few microseconds and opened up this hole."

"There, you see?" said Sylvie. She looked at Marty. "He's coming around."

"Now *I'm* not so sure," said Marty, looking up. "This is an awfully big hole."

"Right," said Zeke. "And what does a normal IO field do when it tries to expand against a couple of extra grams of space dust? It implodes. Bang. Good-bye ship."

Sylvie started to say, "Well, this ship—"

"No," said Bones. "This ship was wrecked on *impact*. In fact, the IO field *preserved* the wreckage."

Marty said, "Then how—"

"I'll tell you what I think," said Bones. "Somebody *did* find the ship. Out there. Sometime between now and a million years from now. They found it and they checked it out and they saw where it was headed—and *when* it was headed—and they saw that the IO was way too old to do the job . . . so they intervened. Like we would if we came across a letter somebody mailed fifty years ago, but it got lost behind a filing cabinet or something. We'd send it along, using whatever modern methods we had."

"That makes sense," said Marty.

"It does." Bones started searching the floor of the chamber.

Keelor Ru said, "They never told me how they aged the bones. I thought they had a lab in orbit. The bones went up, and a couple of weeks later, the bones came back down. Funny thing is, everybody saw them come down, they just didn't know it."

Bones spun around. "A meteor! Exactly! I *knew* that crater was a new feature!"

"Very new," said Sylvie.

"They had to beat the customs people," said Keelor Ru. "By the time the bones were ready, everything had changed. Rumors got out that I had found something: the rebels got hot and the government clamped down."

"I like it," said Marty. "Just send the ship on in and let 'er crash. Retro a cargo package right before impact."

"Destroying the evidence," said Sylvie. "But they didn't count on this IO chamber collecting the pieces."

"They didn't count on the IO at all," said Bones, still kicking around on the curved floor. "The irony is, Bart Charles was so anxious to dump the evidence, he had no idea what he was throwing away. Something worth about a million times whatever he expected to make here on Garu'ka: an IO from the future—more accurate, more reliable, more powerful by far. It was strong enough to open up a hole like this, burning—what?"

"Million kilotons of rock," said Marty, looking around. "A million, easy."

"A prodigious machine," said Bones, bending over. "In a pretty small package, too." He held up a fused piece of metal about the size of a loaf of bread.

Kadak!xa dropped the lander straight down, homing on the emergency beacon. Downlooking radar painted its picture on the screen: a wide, rocky crater at the edge of the Sacred Mound. Its bottom was vaguely convex, and the beacon was right in the middle, getting stronger every second.

Landing gear sprung out of the bottom of the shuttle, fat shock absorbers extended, wide feet twitching, ready to flex around a boulder or dig into a fissure.

"Ten meters," said the computer. "Eight . . . seven meters . . . beacon steady, locked on and centered . . . four meters . . . thrust coming up . . . two meters . . . landing commit . . . one meter . . . signal max . . . thrust at ninety . . . *warning, warning* . . . surface unstable . . . landing commit . . . override enable . . ."

Kadak!xa swore. Her body quivered, spinnerets dribbling silk. "Commit," she said. "Full thrust. Come on, find me some solid ground!"

"Contact," said the computer.

The lander wobbled . . . and continued down.

"Plus five . . . plus seven . . ." said the computer, now reading in centimeters. The lander was sinking into solid ground.

"Thrust override!" said Kadak!xa.

"Landing commit," reminded the computer. "Override denied."

"Emergency. Code . . . uh . . . code Rhinehardt!"

"Plus ten," said the computer. "Landing commit. In the event of a legal override command coming after a reiterated landing commit the procedure must—"

"Hey! Hey! *Listen* to me!" A new voice, full of static blasted from the receiver "Engines off! Engines *off*!"

Kadak!xa killed the engines . . . and the lander dropped like a rock.

Fire burst from the ceiling of the dome, disintegrating the porous crust of rock. Marty was screaming on the radio, but Bones couldn't hear a word. Those engines were LOUD.

A moment later the fire cut off, the sound cut off, and the lander emerged from dust and smoke. It dropped straight down. Bones crouched on the floor of the cavern, hugging the future IO generator as if it would protect him.

On the way back, still savoring his triumph and his revenge, Bart Charles saw, from the gently rolling limo's rear window, the light of Kadak!xa's lander coming down. He smiled, thinking, if that's who I think it is, you're too late. Doc Bones is already dead, crushed under tons and tons of . . .

The lander's heavy feet hit the dirt with a groan, shocks compressing, metal screaming, rocks popping. The wide black, smoking hot exhaust nozzle of the lander's main engine kept right on coming, covering Bones and driving its rim three centimeters into the dirt. The engine bottomed out: pumps cracked, pipes ruptured, and liquid coolant spilled out, covering the outside of the sizzling motor and keeping Bones from roasting to death.

After a long moment the lander rose slowly on its noisy springs, and Bones rolled out from under the lip of the nozzle, over the deep circle of its imprint. He ducked around one of the auxiliary engines and stumbled over a cracked landing pad.

Marty yanked him farther back. "Damn, *look* at yourself," he said. "Your hair's all *frizzy.*"

Bones was still clutching the ruined IO engine. He looked dazed. Marty gave the hunk of metal a friendly pat. "Make a nice paperweight, don't you think?"

It was early in the dark predawn morning when they climbed out of the cracked IO bubble. They had to winch the embarrassed Kadak!xa out with ropes. Professor Digger would remain entombed until the lander was repaired.

"The sky is bright with stars," said Sylvie, "and bright with the promise of a world without war."

"You practicing for your story?" asked Marty.

A whining noise approached them out of the dark night, skimming along the bottom of the crater. Suddenly lights flared and hovered, circling their little group.

"It's Alpha!" said Sylvie. "He found me!"

The camera chirped when she addressed it, and continued to circle.

"I missed you, baby!" said Sylvie. "Did you get some good footage of my abduction? Oooo, I'll bet you did."

"I think I'm going to be sick," said Marty.

Zeke noticed Keelor Ru sitting on the ground, the package of fossils cradled in his lap. He looked content, finally. His part was over.

A lot of people had died for those bones—and for the other ones, the fakes. Million-year-old bones...million-year-old fakes...

"Oh, hell," said Zeke. "I just thought of something horrible."

"*Please* tell us," said Marty. "We need to hear something horrible right now."

"It's my stupid neutrino absorption test," said Bones. "According to it the fakes are—"

"Between two and five billion years old," said Kadak!xa. "I knew you'd like that."

"I did, at first. I thought it meant they'd screwed up, that they'd cooked the bones too long in some neutrino chamber. But I was wrong: the fakes really *are* a million years old."

"So?" said Marty.

"So sometime between now and a million years from now, the

high-energy neutrino flux of the galaxy has got to be a couple thousand times what it is today. That's a lot of exploding stars."

Sylvie laughed. "Universe ends, film at eleven."

"No, really," said Bones. "This is *serious*."

"A million years from now?" said Marty.

"Could be tomorrow," said Bones.

"Speaking of tomorrow," said Merrily, "I really *have* to get home. If my dad finds out . . ."

Bones looked at Marty.

Sylvie put her arm around Merrily's shoulder. "Come on, Red. We got some stuff to talk about."

EPILOGUE

On his first day back under the domes of New Yale, Bones was met in his office by homicide detective McClennan.

"Nice tan," said the cop.

"Thanks."

"Hey, I saw you on the news last week. 'Crisis Averted On Garu'ka,' or something like that. I just tuned in for the ball scores."

Bones nodded, smiling. "How 'bout those Mets?"

"Don't talk to me about it."

McClennan didn't have time to sit down, and that was a good thing, since the chairs and most of the floor were covered with the texts and printouts Zeke had accumulated to prepare for this term's lectures.

"Just thought you'd like to know," said the detective. "We got the guy who killed your friend. Janova?"

Zeke's smile faded. He had been expecting this. "But you'll never be sure, will you?"

"What do you mean?"

"The guy's dead, right?"

"How did you know?"

"That's the way it works, isn't it? Who was he?"

"Itinerant spaceport worker, disappeared the day your friend came through Boston. Found him in a motel on Mars."

"Dead."

"Poisoned."

"Same stuff they used on Janova?"

McClennan nodded.

"Yeah," said Bones. "Some guys have a fondness for irony."

He knew—or thought he knew—the dead spaceport worker was a plant, but there was no point in telling McClennan.

"Off the record," said the detective. "Who's behind all this?"

Zeke shook his head. "I could never prove it."

Like that business on Garu'ka: folks come and go, and when it's all over, nobody remembers who was where or who did what. Right now there were guys ready to swear Bart Charles never left Earth all summer.

"That's not the way I want it," said Bones. "But it's the way it is."

"Yeah, I know." McClennan pulled at the rubberized hood of his coat.

"Is it raining out there?" asked Zeke.

The cop shrugged. "It's always raining somewhere."

TECHNICAL DATA

VISUAL DATA BY
JOEL HAGEN
CHARACTER DESIGN BY
STERANKO

 Dr. Ezekiel Bones had long been aware of the bitter controversy surrounding the origin of intelligent life on the planet Garu'ka. Fragmentary evidence and superficial similarities had led earth to lay claim to Garukan sentients as descendants of an inferior line of *Homo sapiens*.

Bones had never believed the theory. The surface similarities between Garukans and humans were insignificant when compared to their structural differences. And Bones believed that the simplest solution to a problem is most often the correct one. Positing a mysterious alien race that took zoological specimens from one planet and transported them to another was just too complicated and bizarre to be correct.

When the discovery of apparently irrefutable evidence proving Garukan descent from Terrestrial hominids was announced, Bones accepted the challenge of disproving the fossils' authenticity. After viewing them, he was convinced they had been faked. But the standard dating tests confirmed that the Garukan fossils really were 1.2 million years old.

Bones's own theory of Garukan evolution centered on an ancient species of flightless bird, native to the planet. It was this species that gave rise to modern Garukans, according to his theory.

While searching for the flaw in the dating of the newly discovered fossils, Dr. Bones also gathered evidence from the Garukans' own ancestors. They had provided carvings and constructions, in the forms of their ancient temples—carvings that portrayed avian beings, and constructions that bore a resemblance to nests.

These cultural artifacts helped indicate what kinds of fossils he should be looking for, and which he did, eventually, find, settling a xenoanthropological question that might have caused a war.

CATALOGUE OF GARUKAN ANTIQUITIES

BV-29

BONES
DATA BANK
ZB/04

IMAGING SCREEN | BONES
TEMPLE CARVINGS

CATALOGUE
OF GARUKAN
ANTIQUITIES

BV—41

BONES
DATA BANK
ZB/04

| IMAGING SCREEN | BONES |
| TEMPLE CARVINGS | |

LW RADAR PACK-SCAN

MASS-CON INDICATED

BVA-3 | 345.2
NAVCOM LINK

PERSONAL RESEARCH

REF. SHEET 12

BIO-LAYER REMOVED BY COMPUTER

BONES
DATA BANK
ZB/04

| IMAGING SCREEN | BONES |
| TEMPLE MOUND | |

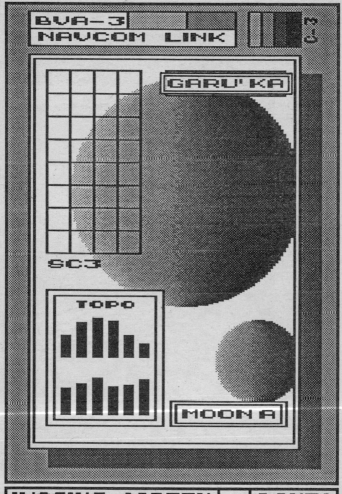

BVA-3
NAVCOM LINK

GARU'KA

SC3

TOPO

MOON A

IMAGING SCREEN   BONES
SIZE COMPARISON

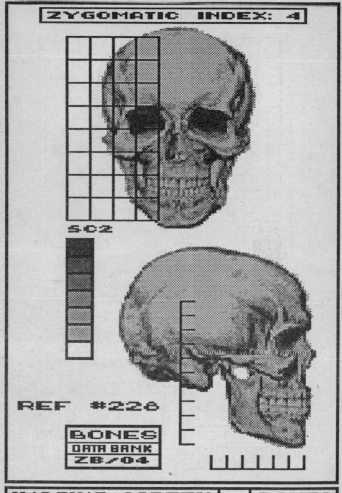

ZYGOMATIC INDEX: 4

SC2

REF #228

BONES
DATA BANK
ZB/04

| IMAGING SCREEN | BONES |
| HUMAN SKULL | |

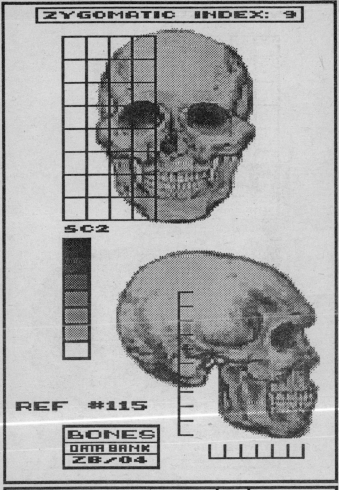

ZYGOMATIC INDEX: 9

SC2

REF #115

BONES
DATA BANK
ZB/04

IMAGING SCREEN   BONES
GARUKAN SKULL

EVA-3

BONES
DATA BANK
ZB/04 ▢ ▢ ▢ ▢ ▢

NAVCOM LINK
1136.4 ACS

NULL VECTOR

IMAGING SCREEN BONES
GARU'KA APPROACH

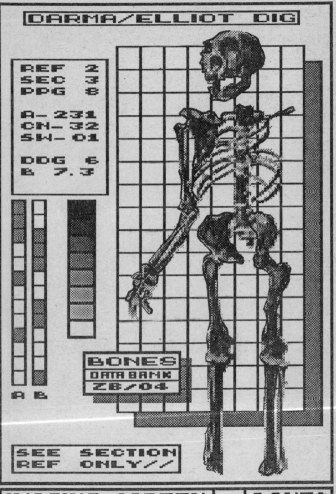

CATALOGUE
OF GARUKAN
ANTIQUITIES

BV—116

BONES
DATA BANK
ZB/04

C2

C4

| IMAGING SCREEN | BONES |
| TEMPLE ENTRANCE | |

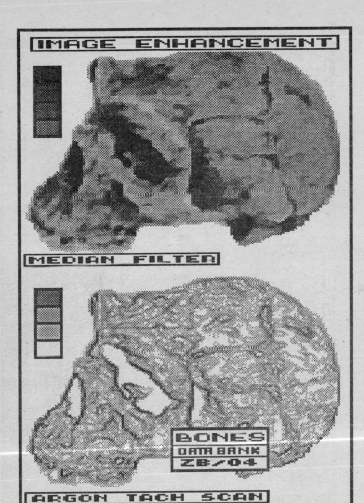

IMAGE ENHANCEMENT

MEDIAN FILTER

BONES
DATA BANK
ZB/04

ARGON TACH SCAN

IMAGING SCREEN	BONES
GARUKAN ANCESTOR	

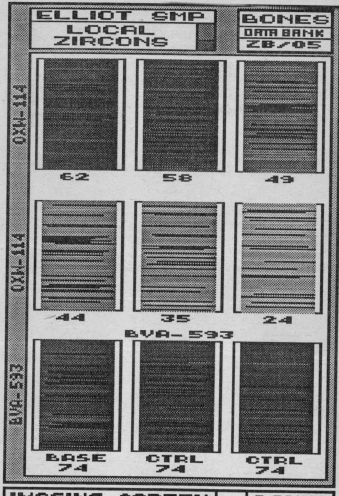

ELLIOT SMP
LOCAL ZIRCONS

BONES
DATA BANK
ZB/05

OXI-114

62   58   49

OXI-114

44   35   24

BVA- 593

BVA-593

BASE   CTRL   CTRL
74   74   74

IMAGING SCREEN   BONES
FISSION TRACK ANALYSIS

CATALOGUE
OF GARUKAN
ANTIQUITIES

BONES
DATA BANK
ZB/04

IMAGING SCREEN		BONES
TEMPLE CARVINGS		